Turn North at the Rim of the World

Book One of Clan Traveler

This is dedicated to the Boy. And his brothers and
sisters everywhere on Mother Earth.

1.The Boy Makes a Friend

A long time ago, when Mother Earth was very young and still infatuated with her Creation, a Boy lived in the woods just outside of a Village. He was tall and skinny, with long wild shiny black hair that had never seen a comb or brush. He had a sweet little nose that any mother would want to kiss, but he had no mother. His hands and feet were too large, and he had bright green almond-shaped eyes that seemed to see everything and nothing at the same time. His eyes were like looking into a clear running stream - they changed all the time. He had no language, so he howled, snorted, muttered and sang what he felt he needed to communicate. Which wasn't much, because he was alone. The folks in the Village felt that he might possibly be a demon - he looked and sounded so strange, and he was fearsome when he chose to howl. So they put out some food for him at night, when their doors and windows were locked, and their children were safely inside.

He did not remember anything about his life before he lived in the woods just outside the Village. He did not know how he came to live there, and he knew nothing about People, save that they did leave food out for him. Sometimes, they left rabbit skins so he could keep warm when it was cold outside. And he understood that they were very afraid of him. From the woods, he watched the people in the Village, and after a while, he noticed that they spoke with each other, hugged, wept, danced, and ate with each other. While he had no language, he did have thought. So he Thought about what he had observed, and he Thought for a long, long time.

Eventually, he decided to leave. He had no idea where he was going, or even why. He just knew that something was speaking to him, and he decided to listen. Because it was Mother Earth speaking, and even without language, he understood what she was telling him.

He simply began walking. His feet were well callused, and he was strong and healthy. He knew what plants he could eat along his way, having survived many years of eating the wrong plants, and finding the right ones. So he just walked towards where he saw the sun setting at night. It was a direction, and direction was what he was seeking.

One day, he saw a scruffy animal picking at a deer carcass. The animal had four legs, a furry coat, bright eyes, alert ears, a happy tail, and a rather long nose. The Boy didn't think the animal was any kind of threat, so he began to speak. He said "Hello" in a kind of singing way. And the animal responded to him. "Hello. I'm called Coyote. I'm not used to humans who can speak to me. Who are you?"

The Boy responded, "I don't know who I am. I lived near a Village, and I lived in the woods. The people there thought I was a demon. I don't look like them, and I cannot speak like them. So I'm searching. I don't know where I'm going, but I am looking to not be alone anymore." He sang this, with a few growls thrown in to emphasize his point.

Coyote responded. "Well, I have yet to meet a Person who can speak with me and make sense. You sing well, and you growl even better. You make sense. Can we travel together?"

The Boy sang, "Yes, I like that. I'm going towards where the Sun goes down."

Coyote said, "Count me in, Boy. Let's go and find some food. And a safe place to sleep."

So the Boy found some berries, and Coyote hunted down a rabbit. Coyote was surprised when he discovered that the Boy could put the rabbit on a stick and cook it over a fire he had made. The Boy also took a sharp rock, skinned the rabbit, and put the skin aside to wear later. When the Coyote asked him why he did this, the Boy just sang that he had seen the People in the village doing this, they could wear the skin to keep them warm, and it

made the meat taste so much better. After a few
bites, Coyote agreed. Although he was really
uncomfortable with the idea of wearing someone
else's skin. That might be all right for the Boy, but
he had his own fur, and he would use that to keep
him warm.. The Boy was obviously hairless, and
Coyote wished him well wearing the skins. He
obviously could not grow a decent pelt on his own.

They slept well at the base of a great tree. The
stars came out, one shy, bright star at a time, and
there was a new moon hanging like a fragile
ornament in the deep blue sky. After a while, it
became cool, and Coyote did what all dogs do, and
snuggled up to the Boy for warmth. The Boy did not
have any memory of ever being snuggled, and
woke up, startled. Coyote slept on. He even snored
a little bit, because it felt so good to snuggle up on
a coolish night. Eventually, the Boy felt a sense of
peace and comfort he had never known before. He
moved in closer to Coyote. He sang a quiet small
song about feeling safe and peaceful into Coyote's
ear. Coyote snored happily. They slept like that
until the Sun came up and the birds began to sing.

The Boy and the Coyote traveled on towards where
the Sun goes down at night. Coyote told the Boy
stories about his pack, playing with his littermates,
learning how to hunt, and learning to stay away
from People. Coyote was amazed that the Boy had
no memory of anything like pack or family. The Boy

was amazed at the love and joy Coyote was describing. They were both in agreement about staying away from People, and when they would see a Village on their travels, they made sure to stay far away.

What had begun as a casual alliance began to grow into a deep friendship. The Boy found good places for berries and green plants he could eat. Coyote had little interest in berries, and no interest at all in green plants that could be eaten. However, he did find the meat he caught that the Boy then cooked on a stick over a fire to be very tasty. He felt that he could perhaps get used to this partnership. The Boy, having never known any kind of companionship, found Coyote to be comforting in many respects. To begin with, Coyote was very funny. He would play gentle little jokes on the Boy. For instance, one day after an especially green plants dominated meal, the Boy burped loudly, as only Boys can do. Coyote burped back, and a burping conversation punctuated by much laughter then happened. At first the Boy found these jokes to be disconcerting, because his life had always been about surviving, certainly not about telling jokes. Soon he found himself looking forward when the next Coyote-inspired joke would happen. In addition to jokes, having someone to sleep next to, or to look at the moon and stars with was also comforting. Finally, being able to talk with anyone, and then being understood for that speaking gave the Boy a sense of relief that was as big as the bright blue sky overhead. Having never known these things, the Boy was opening up and looking at everything with new eyes. For his part, Coyote had been a solitary traveler for his own reasons for a very long time. He discovered that the Boy was endearing in the way that Coyote pups are endearing, although he hoped that the Boy would be able to find a way to becoming something more than a very large and hairless Pup.

2. Coyote Meets The Mountain Behind the Mountain

There was a day when Coyote and the Boy walked through an early Spring thunderstorm. It was not a bad storm, as storms go, and they were enjoying the feeling of the warm water rinsing the dust from their skin, quenching their thirst, and letting them know that the abundance of a good harvest with plenty to eat was coming. After the rain stopped, and the Sun came back out, Coyote decided to take a zooming run. The Boy, not being canid, did not understand the need for Coyote to take a long zooming run, but he watched with a grin as Coyote careened out of sight.

Coyote felt so good that he ran, lept as high as he could, bit at the air, and even howled a little. He was enjoying his life of travel with the Boy. He had lost his pack long ago to trappers - Coyote pelts are

very warm, and winter can be very cold - and he
had had no desire to make a pack again after that.
He had escaped simply because he had been far
afield, foraging for food for his family. When he
came back to what was left, part of him died with
his pack and he decided to spend the rest of his life
in a solitary way. Somehow the Boy reminded him
of his pups. Bumbling, naive, yet intelligent in their
own way. And certainly in need of protection. He
puffed out a little bit - maybe he could take care of
the Boy, and get him to wherever they were going
in one piece. Yes, he could do that. He wanted to
take care of the Boy, and decided at some point
that the Boy was meant to be his new pack. Today,
he had enjoyed the rain, his belly was full, he and
the Boy were becoming friends, so he ran and lept
and howled with no thought about the future.

After a while, he stretched and yawned a squeaky
happy little canid yawn. He smiled, like all canids
know how to smile, and decided that it was time to
trot back to the Boy - he could easily follow the
scent. Slowly, he became aware of a gentle
humming song that was making the new leaves on
the trees shake, leaving him very curious to
discover the source. So he went belly down, and
began to stalk. He heard the running water of a
stream, and the source of the sound was coming
from there. His belly went even lower to the ground,
and he stalked even more slowly. He did not think
that trappers hummed a beautiful sound, but he

also did not wish to find out firsthand. His yellow
eyes were glowing and he was looking straight
forward, while his ears were rotating to all the four
directions, making sure there was no threat from
elsewhere in the woods. He saw a large Oak near
the stream, so he slunk behind it, and very, very
quietly looked out from behind the protection of the
tree.

The first thing he noticed was a tallish Person with
Spring flowers braided through her hair. She wasn't
old, but she wasn't young either. He wasn't sure
what People thought was beautiful (after all, his
standard of beauty was based on Coyote standards
of beauty. In his estimation, she was a lovely
Person…). She was tall, but she moved with a
sure, steady grace that came from many year's
worth of experience walking in the woods. What
was most amazing (and here, Coyote held his
breath in both awe and fear), were the Wolves
travelling with her. Coyote considered Clan Wolf to
be his elders, and while he respected them, he
gave them a wide berth. Coyote was a pretty
talented trickster, and had his own magic - which
he took pride in. That being said, the Clan Wolf was
Big Magic, Earth Magic, and far beyond what
Coyote could comprehend. So he just held his
breath, and hoped the Wolves would not notice
him. Part of him wanted to run away as fast as he
could, but another part of him, that part that still

mourned his pack, wanted to stay and listen to the Person humming her song.

Of course, he hesitated for so long, that the larger of the two Wolves turned his great head, and sniffed. Then he looked directly at Coyote. To Coyote, it was like looking right into the Sun. He did not know if it felt wonderful, or if it meant that his death was imminent. He just held his breath some more, waiting. The Golden Wolf said to his Elder, "Look over there, do you see a trickster? Right there, trying to hide behind that Oak?"

The Silver Elder Wolf was smaller, but no less imposing. He was steady and strong, and had walked beside his Person in dedication for many years. He was an Elder in every good way. "Shhhh…", he growled, "You will frighten that poor little Trickster to death. I can see he is only curious." The Golden Wolf muttered a quiet-under-the-breath-something about how much fun it might be to terminally frighten a Coyote, and his Silver Elder batted him with an affectionate paw. "Hush, now.", he grumbled. "Trickster, please show yourself!" the Silver Elder Wolf barked loudly. His Person, turning slowly from her song, was very curious about what was going on. The lovely Humming had been coming from her, and now it ceased as she waited and watched.

Coyote was shaking, but he came out from behind the Oak. "I apologize deeply." he whimpered, with only a little whining. "I heard the lovely Humming Song and I just wanted to get near it. I don't mean any harm. I have a Person Pup I need to get back to, please. Really, he needs me. Please. I'm not joking. Really. Honestly." Coyote was panting heavily by now, as the two Wolves and the Person regarded him impassionately. Coyote held his breath again and waited.

After what seemed to be at least a year, but was most likely only a few seconds, the Silver Elder Wolf spoke again. His voice was mild, but it also carried an undertone that did not invite any challenge. "So, Trickster. We have seen you before. You're traveling. And with a young Person. It's rather unusual for a Coyote to be keeping company with a Person. Would you kindly tell us more?".

Coyote was so relieved that he was not being turned into a tug-of-war between two very large Wolves , that he just started babbling. He began with losing his pack to the trappers and deciding to live a solitary life, to meeting up with the Boy, who did look strange, that is, until you got to know him, and then he was like a Pup, so he was lovely in Coyote's eyes, and how the Boy was a new way for him, not a new pack, that was gone, but a different one, and maybe the Boy was on to something, he

did listen to the wind at times, and always seemed
to find just the right spots for food and sleep, so, in
other words, Coyote had decided to align himself
with this Boy who was obviously just a very tall and
hairless pup. "So." concluded Coyote breathlessly
and all in a rush, "There it is. I know it sounds
strange. But it's truth. And I need to get back to him
before the Sun goes down." Coyote hesitated,
"Respectfully, I have utmost respect for Clan Wolf. I
just need to get back to my friend. My hairless Pup.
Please."

The Wolves began to converse In low and
grumbling tones with each other. Coyote only
wanted to get back to the Boy. He had had no idea
how deeply he felt about the Boy until his outburst.
Now, it was all he could think about. "Please.
Please. Please. Please." He kept saying this inside
his mind as he listened to the Wolves discourse. "I
want to go back to my pack please." After what
seemed to be far too long for Coyote, the Person
stood up slowly. She had a knife, but it remained
sheathed. It looked like a skinning knife, and
Coyote, remembering what he had returned to felt
the blood pool coldly in his gut, and he felt his heart
stutter a little bit. Like maybe his heart was
expecting to stop sometime soon, and didn't much
like that idea. Coyote looked at her believing he
was now pleading for his life, and not proud of the
fact. Nevertheless, he wanted to get back to the
Boy. And quickly. He would beg, plead, pee, and

go belly up in submission if necessary - after all, a Trickster has the ability to do whatever is necessary in the moment, and to do it well. That is the gift the Trickster brings. So he gathered his mind, and took a deep breath to speak.

Before Coyote could get a word out, she spoke. "Quiet, now. No harm will come to you." she said in a low, even voice. "There is a reason you came here, Trickster." She then whispered to the two Wolves, "Please be quiet, Coyote and I need to talk." They grumbled a bit, but stopped their conversation. Coyote was happy to hear the end of that particular conversation.

The Golden Wolf and the Silver Elder lay down at her side as she sat down on a rock beside the stream. "Come over here, little Trickster, we have something we need to discuss." Her gaze was level, and while not inviting or warm, Coyote breathed a huge breath of relief, knowing he was not in harm's way, and would get back to his hairless Pup with a good tale to tell.

"Coyote, my dear Trickster, there will be no tale to tell your large, hairless Pup." Coyote looked up at her, round-eyed. While he could usually gather the thoughts of most People, this one while seeming to be very kind, was a complete blank slate. Her thoughts were not a constant chatter, they were like a solid clear blue sky with no clouds. "I have a bigger thing to discuss with you, Trickster, and it requires your guidance and your silence. Do I have that?" Coyote felt that total agreement at this point was in everyone's best interests, so he swallowed a whole lot of very dried-up spit, as well as many pounds of pride, and grunted, "You know you do. My silence and my guidance. I swear it." then he added as an afterthought, "On my honor as Clan Coyote."

She laughed then, her shoulders lifted, she shook her hair back, sprinkling flowers everywhere, years of sadness leaving her face. "Coyote!" she laughed," You are a Trickster with honor, and that's a pretty rare thing!" Coyote thought seriously about being deeply offended. He was, after all, Trickster, and that was just his nature. He grumbled a little bit inside his mind that even a Trickster knew about honor. After all, the Boy was now Pack, and one did not dishonor the Pack. Immediately, he realized that his Thinking was transparent to this Person, and he squashed the thought like biting a flea.

Too late. She turned to him, holding his head in her callused and capable hands so his gaze had to meet hers and said, "No offense to Clan Coyote meant, friend. Now. We have to have a conversation,which is why you came here, so get comfortable, set those big ears towards me, and listen to what I am about to tell you."

For once, Coyote chose to not challenge what was obviously someone who held seemingly all the authority in the world. He lay down, keeping a wary eye on both Wolves, and turned his dish-like ears towards her.

She began, half-singing and half-speaking. Coyote was entranced, as he always loved a good story, so he forgot about the two Wolves, and settled into listening with all of his being.

She began, "Sometime far in the future, or deep in the past - depending on where you're standing, a great Person will say, "God does not play dice with the Universe'" Coyote tilted his head, indicating that he really didn't understand. "Well," she said, "What that means is that the Creator does not play Tricks upon Creation. I think you can understand that?"

Coyote sighed. He understood.

"Coyote, your meeting with the Boy was no mistake. And the Boy is no mistake. Like all of Creation, he has a purpose and a path. There is no such thing as scrap in Creation. People who did not understand the Boy's true heart left him at the edge of the Village to wither and die. He did not, because his purpose is much more than that. Clan Coyote was chosen to be his companion because you are smart and resourceful. Like the Boy, you have also lived just outside of the Village, on the edge of things. Like the Boy, you have also been hurt by the People, and it was a hurt you did not earn or deserve. Damaged hearts find each other in order to heal, and the Boy found your heart. You also saw and recognized him as whole in his heart. He is."

Coyote was all ears. He had never felt that he had any individual significance, he was just Trickster. Suddenly, that didn't seem so shameful.

She looked at Coyote with great affection, and gave a little scratch to his rear. Like all canids, Coyote found this delightful. He yipped a little bit in happiness, and then threw a wary look to the two Wolves. They chose to ignore him.

"You are to walk with the Boy to the rim of the World. You will find other walking companions along the way, and they will complete your party. When you are near the rim of the World, you will face a challenge - it is mutable that the Boy will survive. Which is why you are with him. You must remain smart and resourceful. And," she smiled sadly, "you must realize that the outcome is not final yet. It will depend on the Boy, your other companions, and most of all on you, Trickster." Coyote looked at her with deeply pleading eyes. He had seen enough challenges for one life, and he did not want to ever see the Boy in danger. "I know." she replied, "we have all seen enough challenges, but you are uniquely talented to deal with this. That is why you were the Clan and the individual that was chosen. Be sure of yourself. The outcome cannot be seen, but it is known you are the one who can create a good one."

"Who are you?", Coyote barked. The Wolves looked solemnly at him. "Who is speaking here?"

"You know." she said evenly. "I am simply part of the Mountain that is behind the Mountain."

Coyote puzzled on that. He loved a good puzzle and this was a nice, juicy big one. "Hmmmmmm," he sang after a while, "I am thinking that you mean the Spirit Mountain that lives within and behind the Earth Mountain. Did I get right? Did I? I bet I did!"

"Yes." she sighed happily (and Coyote thought with a bit of a sense of relief), "Indeed, you got it right, Coyote. You certainly did."

Coyote was so excited and filled with purpose that he leapt right up into her arms, totally disregarding the two Wolves who were looking at him with a deep sense of amusement. He licked her face like he was a Pup, and he howled and sang like only Coyote can. She sang as well, happy that Coyote now knew his purpose, and his sense of purpose was healing his shredded heart. She finally put him down gently, giving his wriggling rear one more good scratch.

"Now, it is time for you to go back to the Boy. You will find him sleeping safely under a large blue spruce tree a few klicks upstream. You will wake him up gently, and you will proceed on your travels. You are not to speak of this meeting. It is highly not in my nature to interfere, but this was justified. Go Coyote!"

Coyote began to run eagerly to where he knew the Boy was, then turned and halted abruptly. She and the Wolves were moving downstream, fading in the oncoming twilight. "Wait! Wait! Wait!" he barked, "Will you come back? Can I see you again?"

He barely heard her sung reply, "Look at the Mountain behind the Mountain, my friend. We might meet again."

3. Redbird

During this exchange the Boy was sleeping and dreaming. He was dreaming a memory he did not know he had kept. He dreamt of being very small, barely walking. He was hungry, cold, and not comprehending why he was alone at the edge of the woods. He didn't remember how he came to be where he was, and the small beginnings of panic were walking around him like hungry weasels. He heard a song deep within the woods, and started crawling towards it. After a while, he felt he simply could not crawl anymore, and just gave up. He lay face down and exhausted in the dirt, and fell asleep. He woke up quite suddenly to feel a very large, rough and wet tongue licking his face.

In his dreaming Boy yelled, like only a little Person can yell, "Gaaaa! Ickkkk! Gaaaaa!" and other, more incomprehensible sounds that little People make. "Gaaaa!." He rolled over, too afraid to even feel afraid. There was a large, panting, drooling, grinning Animal standing over him. Had the Boy been wearing pants, they would have become very wet. As it was, he just lay there, panting. And very wet.

This Animal was large, and had equally large teeth. As well as the rough and wet tongue that had awakened the Boy. "Gaaaa!" he screamed yet again. Then he began to cry. The teeth came closer. Suddenly that large and very pink tongue descended and began licking his face again. In terror and a great loneliness, the Boy reached up grabbing the fur on the Animal's neck. Apparently that was the right thing to do, and the Animal took off at a fast trot. After what seemed to be a long time, but was really no time at all, they came to a quiet spot within the woods. By this time the Boy had again fallen deeply asleep out of exhaustion. He awoke on the ground, looking into a small and cozy little fire. He smelled something wonderful, and his stomach began to have an anticipatory conversation with the wonderful smell.

Hearing a growl from behind him, he quickly curled up into a tiny ball of a Person. The singing continued, and because he had no People language, the Song spoke to him. He looked up and saw a Child, much older than him, but still a Child. She had bright red hair, a color he had never seen before, and it was chopped in some random pattern all over her head. She was very pale, having translucent skin that was almost colorless in its paleness. Most disconcertingly, she had bright blue eyes that seemed to be taking ruthless measure of the Boy. He stared back at her, wondering if she was even a Person.

"Hello!" she sang brightly and unexpectedly, "I am so glad Storm found you! He has been looking for you for a long time, and I was worried we would not find you." Storm, who was large, wolflike, but most certainly not a wolf silently agreed. The little Girl Person chirped again, "Well, I am happy we found you. Would you like to enjoy some rabbit grilled al fresco? Hormone and antibiotic free, I can assure you. I am thinking you must be feeling simply famished."

The Boy howled back loudly that he was, indeed, hungry. Very hungry. He decided that the weasels of fear had slunk away for a bit, and he might as well make the best of this strange situation. So he ate. When in doubt about one's existence, eat.

After a full and companionable silence, the Girl Person chirped again. In his mind, the Boy was calling her Redbird. Because of her wild red hair. And because she chirped. She seemed to hear that, and smiled. "It has been a very long time since I have had a name.", she chirped. "Redbird is delightful. I accept the name, and thank you very much for it." She laughed a little snorty laugh that the Boy found wonderful, and then said, "Well, not to spout a cliche', but I suppose you're wondering why you're here, and why I have called this meeting."

Indeed, the Boy was full of wonder. Still dreaming, the much older Boy rolled over and got more comfortable in the sweet-smelling pine needles under the blue spruce. There was a smile on his face, as his dream memory continued.

"Little Boy", chirped Redbird, "You have a purpose and a path to walk. When the time is correct, you will find a friend, in fact you will find many friends, and you will go about that purpose. I say so, and I say truth."

The Boy thought about that. All he had known so far had been the People of the Village sometimes putting food out for him, but mostly treating him with fear and avoidance. He turned the thought of having friends around and around and around, like a pebble tumbling in a stream. Eventually, he decided to put that particular thought away for another time. While it seemed to be a very good thing, it was also more than he could really hold onto as a possibility. So he put it away for a while and allowed it to tumble around in the fast-running stream of his mind.

"Indeed!" sang Redbird, "You really are endearing. Even Storm thinks so! Correct, Storm? Please respond, sweetheart." Storm responded with a growl that sounded like low and dangerous thunder from far away. The Boy was not quite so sure that Storm also found him endearing, but was not about to argue the fact.

"So." she continued, "For the time being, Storm and I will be teaching you some survival skills. Please be attentive. This is not a dress rehearsal."

And the Boy was. He learned how to outsmart a rabbit, so he could have meat. Storm taught him that part. Redbird taught him what plants were good food, and what plants to avoid. She also taught him that no matter how good the mushrooms looked, to just not even attempt to eat them, and she spoke from experience.

For her part, Redbird was very happy to have a Name, and to have some company, even for a short time. Like the Boy, she had no real memory of anything other than living in the woods with Storm, a large shaggy-coated Not-Wolf Not-Dog who had always been with her. Unlike the Boy, Redbird was pretty sure she wasn't exactly a Person any longer. She had heard the People of the nearest Village describing her as some sort of wood-spirit, or maybe even a ghost. These thoughts made her even lonelier, so she did not think them often. She felt that her reality was mutable, flexible, neverending, and fluid. This was not a comfort.

After a time, Redbird told the Boy he was to go back to his spot outside the Village and wait. When it was time to move, she chirped brightly, he would know, and he would move towards where the Sun went to sleep. While the Boy did not want to leave, Redbird was adamant. He had work to do, she said, and she had work to be doing as well. Perhaps in the fulfillment of time, they would meet again. Perhaps. Maybe.

Storm took him back to his spot outside the Village. Because he was looking forward when he left, the Boy did not see Redbird walk back alone into the woods, and he never saw the tears running down her face like a little waterfall. He felt he would always remember her with joy as being funny, wise, and a fierce teacher. What he did not know was that while tears were running down her face, she was also singing a song of forgetting - the Boy had his own path to walk, and he now had the skills to walk it.

For a long time the Boy sorely missed Redbird, her sense of purpose as well as her sense of humor. The song, however began to work its magic and then he began to forget, as we all do, and to live within that absence. When he met Coyote, he had felt a sense of something lost being found again. This is because nothing of value to our soul is ever really forgotten - we think we have forgotten, but the memory has simply become part of our being. While the front of his mind had forgotten Red Bird, his soul certainly had not.

In his sleeping, the Boy wondered if Red Bird and Coyote were kin. It seemed plausible. They were both fierce, and they were certainly both funny. He realized this remembering through what seemed to be a dream was important. He snuggled down comfortably again and waited, while dreaming, for his friend Coyote to return.

4. Full Moon Dreams and Thoughts

Loping easily upstream, towards where he knew the Boy was sleeping, Coyote turned what had just occurred over and over in his mind. Life, he decided, was certainly becoming interesting. He had joined the Boy on his travels simply because he was bored and lonely - and now, here he was having mysterious conversations with beings he thought only existed in stories. Eventually, he found the blue spruce the Boy was still sleeping under, and decided that he could use a nap as well. He sighed a happy sigh, made a little circle, and curled up next to the Boy. For his part, the Boy snuggled up to Coyote and smiled in his sleeping. Indeed, life was becoming very interesting.

The full Moon rose, and the world turned blue and silver. Coyote and the Boy, both tired after many days of walking slept on. From the top of her favorite tree, Redbird was staring at the Moon wondering where the Boy was and how he was faring. Somewhere else, the Silver Wolf and the Golden Wolf slept curled up much like Coyote, dreaming their own dreams. The Woman was looking at the same full Moon that Redbird was looking at. She was thinking that the future was always mutable. She sighed, and sent out an encouraging thought to Coyote. She had a feeling he would be needing it.

In yet another Somewhere a young Owl swooped
and dove in the silver sky. She was flying simply for
the joy of flight, and it was beautiful to observe.
Eventually, as the silver blue night faded into a light
blue and gold dawn and she, too, slept.

5. Another Traveler

So the Boy and Coyote continued to follow the path
towards where the Sun went at night. They crossed
some rivers, skirted some sharp-looking mountains,
and avoided several small Villages. They foraged
for food, and Coyote was definitely acquiring a
taste for roast Rabbit. They talked with each other
about many things, but neither one of them
brought up their encounters. The Boy was
remembering bits and pieces of his time with
Redbird - but nothing that was ever a full memory
he could name. However, he was left with a sense
of some sort of history, and he was starting to
wonder what would happen when they got to the
rim of the world. For him, it was a new thing to be
living in a world that had a past and a future - not
simply a never ending present. For his part, Coyote
was still in amazement over his conversation with
the Woman. Amazement over the Woman, and
awe over those two Wolves. He didn't really know
how to even begin to discuss the encounter, so he
just didn't. Their days passed pleasantly, and they
felt a sense of purpose. They were going
somewhere, and then that purpose would become
manifest.

The weather remained mild, with just enough rain
to ensure a good harvest. They slept outside at
night without making a shelter, usually under a
friendly tree. On this night, Coyote was wide

awake. He was missing being a part of a pack. As usual, his emotions had snuck up on him and surprised him. So he lay next to the Boy trying to simultaneously ignore his emotions and yet to explore them. He felt a need to Howl, something he had not done in a long time. He did not want to wake the Boy, so he trotted out into a meadow under the bright stars. And he Howled. He put his heart and soul into it, and his Howl rang through the night. He Howled about this journey he was on, he howled about the delights of cooked rabbit, and he howled about the necessity of the Pack. Finally, he sighed, feeling much better, and trotted back to the Boy. The Boy had been awakened by the Howling, and knew it was his friend Coyote. He listened, feeling his heart full of love for his friend, and what his friend had lost. He wondered about Family and Pack, never having known either. Maybe that was what this journey was about, he thought. Maybe. When Coyote returned, the Boy ruffled his fur, and scratched his ears while hugging him tightly. They were friends indeed, and both felt that they were the better for that.

They lay together under the tree sheltering them, watching the stars roll through the night sky. They grew drowsy. They heard a gentle "whoo-hoo!", and thought it a lovely sound. Then they heard a soft whooshing of wings, and a gentle thud. This woke them up again completely,and the two listened for more. They heard a very gentle and sad-sounding "whoo-hoo!", and their curiosity got the better of their caution, so they went to investigate.

Tangled in a blackberry bush was a very young female Owl. She stared at them with huge eyes that reminded the Boy of two small glowing Moons. She shrieked. The Boy and Coyote jumped. She shrieked again, but this time they realized that she was afraid. Both of them knew how awful being afraid feels, so they approached her slowly. She watched solemnly, not knowing what to think. She had seen People and Coyotes before, but never together, and certainly never in the deepest part of the night in the woods.

Coyote said, "Friend Owl, we will not harm you. We are two travelers walking to where the Sun goes to sleep at the rim of the world."

"Let me untangle you." whispered the Boy. "Those blackberry bushes have delicious berries, but they are no fun to get tangled up in, I'll help you."

When she was extricated from the blackberry bush, Owl looked at them and sighed. "Thanks, that was my first flight, and it really did not go well." And another sigh. "I'm not good at this solitary night flying thing. Besides, I'm lost. All these trees look alike to me." The Boy stared at her in amazement. He had heard stories about the mighty hunters of Clan Owl, and the wisdom they were well-known for. This little fluffy Owl did not appear to be either a mighty hunter, or wise. She was rather small, and white, with a dish shaped arrangement of feathers around her face, and enormous deep and glowing eyes that held deep mystery and were transparent at the same time.

Coyote felt the same, but being Coyote he simply blurted out in a rush, "Clan Owl are supposed to be mighty hunters and wise like shamans. What's with you? You tumbled into a blackberry bush, you're lost, and I will bet your belly's empty, too."

Owl was not offended. She hung her head, and her lower beak trembled a little. "You're right, Coyote." she snuffled, "I'm not very good at this wise and mighty hunter thing." Then she added quietly, "And yes, I am hungry. As well as lonely. And a little bit scared."

Well, the Boy and Coyote certainly knew what all that felt like. The Boy had a sudden, fleeting picture of sitting by the fire with Redbird, feeling safe and warm with a very full belly. He said slowly, "Owl, we are traveling. When we get to the Rim of the World, I am thinking we will learn why. Why don't you join us? I know nothing about being an Owl, but then, I know nothing about being a Person, either. So we're even. Come with us."

"Please say yes!" echoed Coyote, leaping up and snapping the air with joy. "We will then be three, and as the saying goes, three makes it a Pack! A Pack would be so nice. Yes, come with us!"

The Boy added, "You can ride on my shoulder, or on Coyote's back when we travel during the day. And you can keep watch at night." He waved away Coyote's stink-eye over this offering of Coyote's back as a perch, and continued, "Coyote is right, it would be nice to be a Pack, please join us!"

So, Owl became the third traveler. She was barely out of the nest, and unsure of her abilities, but the Boy assured her that he too, had been in the same situation - and all alone as well. She spoke to them about Clan Owl, how fiercely and deeply they love, for one thing. She also talked about celebrating the night, the nuances and shades that most never get to see. She spoke about flying far, far up, and then diving down through the sky for the sheer joy of it. The Boy and Coyote listened, totally entranced by her stories about Clan Owl. She was so much wiser than she thought herself to be, they agreed privately. They also thought that "whoo-hoo!" was a very lovely sound, and they enjoyed hearing it at night knowing Owl stood (or rather perched and flew) watch.

6. A Person Named Duck

There are many Somewheres, most of them are wonderful places, some of them are awe-inspiring, many of them are beautiful - and some of them just aren't any of that. In a Village Somewhere, Sometime ago, a child was born. In his birthing, his mother died. When the child was brought before his father, his father rejected the infant as the offspring of a demon. You see, this child was as white as snow that never melts, and his eyes were a transparent pink color. His father asked the midwives to please take the monstrous thing away, and drown it in the river nearby. The midwives, being bringers of life and not destroyers of life, refused his request. They didn't know what else to do, so they brought the child up themselves, with the child spending one moon in each of their homes. As the child grew, people began to notice that he was more than just an eerie skin color. He was becoming not very tall, as People go, but very large. His feet never really caught up with the rest of his body, so he walked by rolling his weight from side-to-side. In other words, he waddled. Like a Duck. So that became his name.

Like the Boy, Duck did not really belong to his Village. He was fed and housed, but nobody ever looked lovingly into his eyes, because his bright pink eyes were so strange they were rather fearsome. His white, white skin was always red and blistered from the Sun, so he was in constant pain. Food seemed to be the only thing that made some of that pain easier, so he ate and ate. Duck's life crawled along in quiet misery. Until the day that he discovered that he could frighten People and get his way. He came to love this power as much as he loved food. Sometimes he would walk right into homes in the darkest part of the night and start screaming like the demon everyone felt he was. "Give me all of your food, or I will eat your children!" he would wail, secretly laughing inside at how gullible People could be. Duck did not have the strength to kill an ant, let alone another Person. "Give me your belongings or I will punch your house down." He would scream, and People being so deeply fearful of him, would comply.

After many years of this, Duck illegitimately grew into Power in this Village. His rage and his demands bent and broke the People of this Village until it became normal and desirable to give him what he wanted in order to escape his wrath. Sometimes Traders would come to the Village. They were not afraid of Duck at all, and told the People so. "He's just a very large and spoiled child.",they would say. "Just ignore him, and he will stop acting this way." The People refused, and told the Traders that Duck was a demigod, and must be appeased. The Traders laughed at this ignorance, and knowing how stupid these People were, always charged them more for things than they charged

other Villages where more loving and intelligent
People lived.

When Duck overheard these conversations with the
Traders, he became deeply frightened. If the
People in his Village saw the real Duck, who was
really only a miserable child no one had ever
wanted or loved, they would laugh at him. Duck had
not only come to love his ill-gained power, he had
come to need it. There was no way he was going to
give it up and have the People of the Village see
the real Duck.

Duck was not wise, but he was sly. Out of that
slyness, he grew a plan to keep things just the way
they were. So he started talking to the People in
groups, stomping his underdeveloped feet so hard
he would almost tip himself over while making
strange and occult hand signals in the air as he
spoke. The People did not realize that Duck had
simply made these strange hand wavings up, and
sincerely believed that the hand-wavings had
magical powers. The People began to look upon
him as a shaman - Duck encouraged that, and
often alluded to having powers the People knew
nothing about. Somehow, this was by far the most
terrifying aspect of Duck the People had yet
witnessed.

He decided to spread his new authority to the
People relentlessly. "These Traders are evil." he

shouted at the top of his voice. "They tell you lies! Lies! They have nothing good to offer you!" he shrieked. Finally, he told the People his biggest lie of all, and this lie was so gigantic that the People of his Village just swallowed it whole. He told the Village that they, the residents of this particular, blessed and special Village were the only People who mattered - any other People that came into this Village were deeply flawed, not really people at all, and needed to be either killed or enslaved.

He taught them a chant. Because People chanting together carries great power. It was simple, yet very strong. It went like this:

"Blood and Fire! Fire and Blood! Protect the Village First and Always! Blood and Fire! Fire and Blood!" The People took it as faith, and chanted it all the time. This made Duck very happy, and also feeling very secure.

Why the People of this Village swallowed these lies and came to live them was a mystery that even Mother Earth could not solve. She watched in slow horror as this Village did, indeed enslave and even kill other People to comply with Duck's fearful and angry words. She wept, and the heavy rains caused the crops to rot in the fields and go unharvested. She shook with rage, and so the Village shook and needed to be rebuilt many, many times. She felt sick and feverish, and the Village

became unbearably hot, fires happened
everywhere, and the water became bad to drink so
everyone felt sick all of the time. They forgot what
feeling free and healthy was like. In short, the
Village was slowly dying, but the People had long
ago forgotten about listening to and respecting
Earth Mother, listening only to Duck telling them
how unique, special, and glorious they were. Duck
told them that Mother Earth was not real, and that
he had the solution to all of these tribulations. The
solution was always the same. Fire and blood,
blood and fire.

Duck was very determined to keep this untruth that
was serving him so well alive,so he told the Village
they needed to set guards daytime and nighttime all
around the outside of the village. So nobody could
get in. If they did somehow get in, Duck would
either have them killed or, if they were young
enough, they could become slaves. If they were
Traders, they could silently sell their goods, but
Duck had to get a cut from the profit on their goods
or they would be banned from the Village. In
response, the Traders simply raised their prices,
but Duck never knew that. The high prices made it
hard for the People to barter things from the
Traders, but they never complained.

Through all of this, Duck was becoming more and
more infirm, in his body as well as his mind. His
white, white skin seemed to always be blistered

and red from any light at all. His eyes were equally painful. His only solace was bullying the village into obeying him, and eating. He became larger and larger, until he could barely waddle. He decided to take some of the child slaves for his own use, and had them carry him around, so his tiny (and by now very sore) feet never had to touch the ground.

Midsummer came, and on the day when the light was the longest, Duck decided to deliver a message. To everyone. To the Mother Earth, to the Sun, the Moon, the Stars, the Wind and the Water. Duck wanted the entire cosmos to bow to him, and him alone. He had himself carried to a large flat rock that the Village used as a central meeting place. There were a few Traders there, as well as some of the People of the Village. By now, while everyone obeyed Duck - because it was certain death to not do so, they were weary of his babbling nonsense and his hatred of anything that was not of Duck. Everyone eyed him warily as he stood, wobbling slightly on the rock.

He began by ranting, screaming and shouting at the top of his voice. None of it was coherent, but the message was plain: Duck had decided that not only did this Village and the People in it belong to him, the entire cosmos was his by divine right. He was not only a demigod, he shouted, he was supreme ruler over Mother Earth. The Sun, the Moon, the Stars, the Wind and the Water were to obey him, and to have no will of their own. The People watched and listened, and while none of it really made any sense, they were also seduced by the idea of owning Mother Earth. They were transfixed by the idea that the Sun, the Moon, the Stars, the Wind, and the Water could be commanded. So they listened silently.

The Traders were appalled by this violation of the order of things, and they quietly packed up their wares, deciding to never return to this Village. Not only was Duck vile and insane,most of the People by continually bowing to his petulant and angry will, had also become insane. The ones that were still sane were sad and silent, hoping this nightmare would end soon. They were no longer aware of the natural rhythm and order of the universe. While the trading had been profitable, the Traders felt it was simply too dangerous to ever set foot in this Village again.

In a different Somewhere, the Woman was tending her garden while the two Wolves slept in the shade. She stood barefoot, enjoying the feel of the Earth under her feet. She loved the order and rhythm of the seasons, and she loved her garden and the good food it produced. Slowly, she became aware of a tremor, a shaking, a silent heaving. She stood very still, listening to it with her whole body, and she realized Mother Earth was weeping. It was coming from the West, and it was unbearably sad.

The Wolves awoke and were also listening, ears up and scanning. Something was dreadfully wrong, and the Woman whispered a quiet prayer for Mother Earth. And for her friend, Coyote as well. The mutable future was rapidly becoming immutable, and she was afraid.

Redbird was far above the ground sitting in her favorite tree when she too, heard the weeping of Mother Earth. Carried on the Wind, it was a soft keening, and the saddest thing Redbird had ever heard. She felt that something terrible must be approaching. She saw burning lakes and sterile forests. She saw starvation and disease. She saw a future that was evil. She wept silently up in her tree, hoping her vision was not a true one.

Duck ranted his nonsense for hours and hours - once started, the fire of his madness and hatred could not be quenched. The People in the Village could not turn away, and they descended into this madness along with Duck. They too began shouting and ranting, feeding Duck's ego right back.

And this continued far into the shortest night of the year.

7.The Boy is Stolen

The Boy, Coyote, and Owl continued on. They felt a
sense of expectation, a sense of urgency, and the
sort of feeling one gets when the sky is clear, but
you know a storm is approaching. Coyote was
uneasy, it was an itch in his mind he just could not
reach to scratch. The Boy felt it as well, and had
taken up awakening in the deep night, thinking he
had heard something. Owl felt something in the
wind as she flew and hunted through the night.
Being good friends, they discussed this. Maybe
they should just stop and settle where they were?
Finally, they decided that they were being pulled by
something they did not understand, and that it
needed to be obeyed.

So they padded on through the forest, always
continuing West towards where the Sun went
down to sleep.

Coyote heard another Coyote yipping nearby, and
started turning his ears to catch where it was
coming from. It did not sound like any from Clan
Coyote he had ever heard before, and he was
uneasy. Just as he was going to comment on this
to the Boy, a rock came flying out of the woods,
hitting the Boy on the back of his head. He fell to
the ground in one fluid boneless motion and lay
still. Coyote looked up from the Boy to see what
seemed to be ghosts flowing silently towards them.

He and Owl melted back into the safety of the woods, watching.

They saw the Boy surrounded by many People. They had seemed to be ghosts because they had painted their faces a corpse-like shade of white. They were loud and angry, calling the Boy a demon, and discussing what they should do with him. Finally, they decided to put him in a cave, guard the entrance, and show him to the head of the Village. The largest of them picked the Boy up as if he were a small child, slung him over his shoulder, and they moved off into the forest. Coyote and Owl followed as quietly as they could (which is to say, very, very quietly…).

Perched up on the top of her most favorite tree, Redbird felt a cold shadow move through her. She cried even more, hoping her vision would prove false. Far below her, resting beneath the tree, Storm began to whine and twitch in his sleep.

While working in her garden, the Woman saw her two Wolves slowly get up and begin to howl. Low and sad. She sent a prayer out to Coyote. She felt fear in the earth under her feet.

8.The Cave, Plans for the Boy's Future, and we meet Duck Again

Coyote and Owl followed this strange entourage to the outer perimeter of a Village. They stayed as far back as they could. Owl watched everything, and Coyote was thinking hard as he padded along. This was most certainly not their purpose, and there needed to be a way to set things right again.

Meanwhile, the People carrying the Boy were chanting "Blood and fire! Fire and blood!" over and over and over. While Coyote and Owl were both carnivores, neither one felt that shedding blood just for the sake of shedding blood was even close to normal. They had never had an exactly warm relationship with People, and they found their feelings towards most people (here Coyote thought of the Woman and her Wolves, and leaping into her arms like a crazy Pup, while Owl was remembering how gently and lovingly the Boy extricated her from the blackberry bush…) getting colder and colder, like a sliver of ice driven into their hearts.

Eventually, the People carrying the still unconscious Boy came to the cave they had spoken of. It was the place they held anyone treading on their sacred Village land until Duck decided what was to be done with that Person. Generally speaking, whatever was chosen wasn't good. They threw the Boy into the cave and several of them stood outside the entrance while Duck was summoned to see the latest interloper.

As the Sun was going to sleep, Duck finally rolled in, carried by his child-slaves in a big (and very heavy) hammock. His white, white skin looked even more painful than ever red, and blistered, while his bright pink eyes were by now totally mad. Nobody could look him straight in the eye and come away feeling clean. He was shrieking, and sounding like a Duck as well as looking like one.

"We have a Demon?" he shrieked and quacked at the same time. "What an accomplishment, my brave Border Guards! A real Demon!" While the Guards had their doubts about the Boy really being a Demon (after all, he had been pretty easy to succumb to capture. Not Demon-ish at all.), they kept silent about their doubts. "You are the bravest and the best! I, Duck, Ruler of All Things say so!" The guards by now, were hoping there was something in it for them - Duck was painful to listen to, after all. "He will be burnt at the stake at dawn! Everyone in the Village must come and watch and learn what happens to those who oppose Duck's rule!" Again, the Guards kept quiet. They were not about to point out that the Boy had simply been waking quietly through the Woods, and really did not seem to pose any kind of threat at all.

But then Duck got into What Was In It For Them. "Brave Border Guards! Bravest of the Brave! Smartest and almost as smart as I, Duck! You deserve a reward!" At this the Guards smiled a little bit. This was feeling better, and they could endure Duck's voice a bit longer. "There is a new and wonderful batch of Ale that I, Duck, had commissioned for my own personal use - I will allow my brave Border Guards to enjoy it, and will have it brought here while you stand watch over the evil Demon who was trying to infiltrate our fair Village. There is also a batch of Mead, very special Mead, the best mead, made especially for me, Duck! I will be generous enough to share it with my brave Border Guards!" At this, the Guards really grinned. Not only had they taken down a defenseless young Boy, they were getting rewarded for it. Not bad, they thought, not bad at all.

9. A Song of Ale and Mead

So the brave Border Guards sat back against the sun-warmed rocks outside of the cave holding the Boy, and waited for Ale and Mead. They were quite pleased with themselves and were doing a lot of back-slapping and fist-bumping.

They were so enjoying themselves that they did not see Coyote and Owl staring at them from the edge of the woods.

Being totally unaware of anything outside of their small experience, they were certainly not aware that there were others listening.

Up in her tree, Redbird heard the speech about Ale and Mead. All of the Earth heard it, and Redbird was pretty pleased that Duck was so incredibly loud. Hearing him rant gave her an idea, and she began constructing a Song. Constructing a Song, a Story, and or any other sort of magic is not as easy as it looks. It looks so pretty from the outside, but the person looking or listening doesn't really know the inside of how it came to be. In Redbird's Song, she drew on a lifetime of watching People, but never really belonging. Sometimes, she thought about trying to belong, but then thought better of it. At the end of the day, most People did not have half the spirit of the Boy, and were small and petty in their being. They were boring and painful to her, and while the loneliness was sometimes very heavy, it was better than trying to be something she wasn't.

She began working on a song.

Somewhere else, the Wolves stopped howling, and turned to look at the Woman. She also was thinking of a Song, but she was not sure what Song to create. She sighed, and went back to furiously weeding her garden. It would come to her, and she hoped that it came in time.

10. In the Cave

The Boy woke up with an aching head, and not knowing where he was. It was dark, he heard people chanting "Fire and blood! Blood and fire!" over and over, and he was deeply frightened. He did not know exactly what had happened, but he knew that it wasn't good. He heard a high-pitched, raspy, rambling voice talking about a Demon, and what should happen to a Demon. It dawned on him quickly that he was the "demon" being spoken about.

The Boy thought, and he thought hard. What would Coyote do? Well, Coyote would either tell a joke, or play a trick. This was no place for a joke, thought the Boy. But the Boy could play a trick, he could pretend to still be unconscious. So he took a deep breath, and made himself go as limp as he could. That was hard to do because he was so scared - but he managed to do it. What would Owl do? Owl could soar effortlessly up into the night sky. Well, thought the Boy, flying wasn't an option. But Owl always watched very quietly and her large moonlike eyes saw everything. So, the Boy opened his eyes to tiny slits. What he saw was amazing and awful at the same time.

He saw a group of people with ghastly white painted faces. He saw them drinking ale and mead while watching and listening to the most horrible being the Boy had ever seen. It took him a while to figure out that it was some kind of Person, but certainly not one the Boy had ever seen before. It was hideously huge, rolls and rolls of fat obscuring the body underneath. It was as white as any snow the Boy had ever seen, yet most of the whiteness was covered in oozing, cracking blisters. Two tiny glaring red eyes were stuck deeply in the bloated and angry face like an afterthought. It was wobbling wildly, as it made odd and occult looking gestures in the air. The Boy was so horrified by this being that he had to force himself to continue to watch and lie still. Because every nerve in his body was screaming at him to run away. However, he knew that would mean his death. The angry crowd of People outside of the cave would simply tear him apart. He would need to know as much as he could learn if he was going to get out of this alive. So his mind went into a quiet space, and he lay on the floor of the cave, watching and listening.

There was someone else there who was watching and listening as well. A young woman who would not paint her face white in deference to Duck was sitting on a large rock observing the festivities. Her name was Corazon, which means "heart". And that described her perfectly. She was a healer in the Village, and other Villages as well. She was not well-loved in her Village because she spoke her truth and would not paint her face, but she was respected because she was a powerful Healer. While her Village and the adoration of Duck broke her heart - she stayed, hoping for the day her People would see Duck for what he really was. Which is to say to see a broken and sick Person who could not wear power without becoming corrupted and vile. She also knew who the Boy was. Because she had seen others like him in other Villages. The Boy was not a Demon at all. He was a rarity, yes, but there were others like him. She cared for these children, teaching them to speak, teaching them to love, and healing the division in their minds. There was nothing evil or wrong about the Boy - in fact, Mother Earth created these rare People to teach others about love and all the different beings she loved. Corazon's big heart was breaking as she listened to Duck ranting and her People chanting.

Corazon was also one of those People who could see the Mountain behind the Mountain, and she knew there were bigger presences on the Earth than what was apparent to eyes and mind alone . She felt the wind rippling through her long dark hair and cooling her lovely brown skin. Slowly slipping into her mind, carried on the wind, she began to hear an odd, but compelling Song. She felt the rippling of Magic surrounding her and everyone else. Being a sensible Person, she listened and watched.

12. A Song of Ale and Mead

Redbird had remained up at the very top of her favorite tree, singing her heart out. She was swaying with the wind, and pushing her Song as far as she could. This just had to work, and she was going to give it her best. She sang about cool, fizzy Ale. How nicely it went down your throat, and how well it would quench your thirst. She sang about how mead tasted like sunshine and summer. How it fuzzed up reality and left you happier than you were - at least for a while. She sang until she simply could not use her voice anymore. Then she clambered down from the tree, sat down next to Storm, and waited. She'd know sooner or later if her Song had worked.

In the clearing, Corazon heard the song, and was watching with humor and amazement. The People were drinking and drinking and drinking. She had never seen so much ale and mead consumed. After a time, they were all the best of friends, hugging and laughing. Singing loudly and off-key together. Stumbling, falling down, and laughing even more. This went on for hours, and Corazon just kept watching, wondering if perhaps, maybe, there could be a chance for the Boy. Like Redbird, she waited.

In the dark cave, the Boy was also watching and waiting. He had survived on his own for many years, and his senses were keen. While he had never seen a group of people consuming so much mead and ale, he knew enough to know what the outcome could be. He also watched and waited.

Finally, when the Moon was at the top of the Sky, all of the People were sleeping in a mead and ale-induced deep slumber. Loud snores and burps rolled through the night, and Corazon had a fleeting thought about churning stomachs and aching heads in the morning, but she really did not care. She saw a chance for the Boy, and she whispered a thank you to whomever had created that song. She moved quickly towards the cave, stepping lightly over snoring and burping sleeping people.

Slipping into the cave, she let her eyes adjust to the deep darkness. She saw the Boy lying quietly, and knelt beside him. For his part, the Boy was beyond terror. He just began to shake and cry. He couldn't help it. He had finally had enough - he was only a Boy, after all. And he just so wanted to be laying under a tree with Coyote looking up at the stars and telling bad jokes. The tears ran down his face, and he just looked at Corazon.

Corazon's heart broke again. She wanted to hold the Boy, and just let him cry himself out but she felt she had to act quickly, before the People began to wake up. "Hush." she whispered. "I won't hurt you, I promise. I know others like you, and I will not harm

you." She knelt down next to him. "Can you talk?"
The Boy could not speak much People-speak, but
he could nod or shake his head. He shook a "no",
his long hair flying around his face.

"That's fine." she said, "I can ask questions, and
you can answer yes or no. Got that?"

The Boy nodded, feeling a little bit of hope.

"Did you come here with others?" she asked. The
Boy nodded.

"Are you going somewhere?" Again, a nod.

"Are your friends waiting for you?" The Boy didn't
know for sure, but he could not imagine Owl and
Coyote not waiting for him, so he nodded.

"Then let's find them! Let's go, and go quickly! I do
not know how this happened, but we'll use it and
get you back to your friends. Please, you can be
just a little bit more brave, you are such a brave
and smart Boy!" This made the Boy smile a tiny and
very shy smile. Nobody had ever called him brave
and smart, and he rather liked it. He stood up
shakily, his head pounding. He looked anxiously at
the soundly sleeping People, but he held out his
hand to Corazon.

They slipped silently out of the cave. They tiptoed around snoring and burping People. They got a few steps into the woods when a furry shape came flying out of nowhere towards them. Corazon hesitated, but the Boy recognized his friend Coyote, and leapt to meet him. They tumbled together in a joyously incoherent heap, while Owl swooped and dove overhead.

Corazon was filled with happiness and awe. While she knew magic, she rarely saw it manifest so strongly. Magic always heals us, and Corazon felt a deep sadness she did not know she carried lift from her. She knew her place was in her Village, but, for a moment, she envied the Boy and his traveling life. She stepped forward, and said, "Boy, I have to go back to my People. I don't like them much right now, but I am needed, and I hope they can change their ways. Travel well!"

The Boy turned, and his strange slanted eyes filled with tears. He had never experienced kindness from a Person before, and this was a big feeling - so People could be kind, after all. That was a huge thought for him, and he would have to turn it over in his mind for a while. Coyote felt the same. He didn't have much use for People, but this girl was different somehow. Like the Woman and her Wolves, he thought fondly. He looked at her, wagging his tail and gave a yip of approval.

She laughed at this, although her eyes were filled with tears as well. "Go!" she whispered, "Get out of this place. Maybe we meet again, maybe not. But you give me hope, something I really needed. Now go!" she hugged them both, waved a farewell to Owl, and ran quickly back to the sleeping People. She had a feeling that the morning would bring a big demand for headache cures, as well as peppermint tea for upset stomachs, and she wanted to get to work.

Corazon went back to the gathering area by the cave shortly after dawn. She had her herbs with her, and she also brought several cloths to wet in a nearby stream. Just as she'd supposed, some up the People were already awake - and they were, as she had predicted, in a world of hurt. They saw her approaching crying out "Me first!", "No me!", "Corazon, my head hurts so badly, I'm afraid it will explode, help me!", and "Oh, Corazon, my belly is so unhappy! Help me!"

She was so busy, and the People were so needy, that no one saw or heard Duck approaching. Until the screeching began. Then they all sat up quickly, and Corazon wanted to run away as far and fast as she could. Duck was never kind to her, although he asked for her frequently. She always dreaded those visits, because she could not help Duck. He refused to cover his body in mud to shield his skin from the sun, and he plugged his hands into his ears when she tried to talk to him about healthy food while he gorged on greasy meat and sweets. She began to move quietly backwards and stood at the edge of the woods, watching.

Duck was more than angry. He felt a rage that made the sun look like a little campfire. His great benevolence, he saw, had been abused. He noticed that there was no one standing guard at the entrance to the cave, and that enraged him even more. "Where is the Demon?" he rasped and wheezed. "Where is he? Answer! Answer!"

There was not one person in the crowd who would look Duck in the eye and answer.
He sent one of the child slaves into the cave, and the child came back out while everyone seemed to not breathe. In a high, true voice, the child said. "Master of the Known and Unknown World, Duck the First of his Name, uh, there isn't anyone in the cave. Well, uh. Just. It's empty. I saw nothing." The child slave stood back, awaiting a blow that fortunately, never came.

Duck rolled out of his hammock and pushed up onto his tiny and painful feet. He started screaming and screaming. And screaming. Then he began screaming some more. He screamed so loudly he felt the blood pooling in his throat, and he did not care. He said terrible things to the People. He vowed to torture and kill all of them. He vowed to throw their children to the Wolves (not knowing that Clan Wolf would take care of those children, and teach them the way of their clan. There are many from Clan Wolf among us - you just need to have the right eyes to see them.). He vowed to take all of their food and let them starve while he gorged. It was terrible to listen to, and the People cowered, cringed, and cried. It went on and on and on.

In fact, it was so terrible, going on for so long, that the Woman and her Wolves heard it. Every word. The Woman was working in her garden, harvesting some especially fine tomatoes she was going to dry for the Winter. In fact, she was enjoying one she had just picked for herself when Duck's tirade was heard on the wind. She was finally fed up with Duck, and his ravaging and raping of Mother Earth. She threw the lovely tomato in fury, spattering it against a tree. The Wolves looked up at her. They had never seen her like this, and they were unsure about what to do. Being unsure, they fell back on a sure thing. They began to howl.

And so did the Woman. She roared out her rage over Duck's violation and blatant lack of respect for Mother Earth. She threw her face up to the sky and shook her fists. She stomped out a dance of fury and sorrow. And finally, it all turned into a Song.

It was a true song, and being true, it became magic. She sang about People taking our Mother back from Duck. A song about loving Her, and treating Her with reverence. She sang a song about People being unafraid to be who they really were, and children never, never being slaves. She sang about People together achieving great things, while People alone were lost. She sang about healing. She sang in a true voice that carried throughout Mother Earth.

Corazon felt the power of the Woman's Voice moving through her bare feet, up her spine, and finally, out of her mouth. She sang along with the Woman, not knowing what she was singing, but trusting totally and singing as loudly and strongly as she could.

Then something occurred that nobody ever really understood. In fact, they never spoke of it among themselves. The People began standing up. Clutching churning bellies and aching heads, nonetheless, they stood up. They took the cloths that Corazon had brought. They went to the nearby stream, dipped the cloths, and began, one by one to wipe the white paint from their faces. Their beautiful brown skin became visible again, and they were looking at each other with love and a sense of unity. There was hugging and laughing and fist-bumping. The child slaves were taken away from Duck by the midwives. They were held and rocked as they wept. The midwives wept as well.

This song rolled on and on. It was a powerful storm of a song, and the People drank it up like thirsty plants. They needed this song, they welcomed it. They looked around at what had happened in their Village, feeling shame. But the song was not about shame, it was about fixing. It was about hoping. It was about creating. The people shook off their shame like Coyote shaking himself off after swimming in a clear, clean stream. Like Owl diving through a rain cloud. Like the Boy running through a cool sun-shower on a hot day. And they began to look at changing things.

Duck was watching all of this. His hot, red eyes missed nothing. He felt a hollowness in his belly that no amount of food could ever fill. What was left of his mind was breaking apart like a puffball mushroom when it gets stepped on. It was flying everywhere.

Some of the People were now also hearing the Woman's song of love and power. They began singing along with Corazon. Eventually, all of the People, their clean faces shining, were turning toward Duck and singing. It was a beautiful thing to hear, and although they never spoke of it again, all of the People held that song in their hearts, passing it along for generations.

Duck could not face this. His plans were ruined, he was ruined, and now the People were looking at

him with truth in their looking. His hold on sanity
had always been fragile at best. Now it finally caved
in on itself, and Duck just broke. He no longer knew
who he was. He no longer cared. He was like a
rabid animal, and he ran howling into the woods.
No one followed him.

13. Owl Becomes Wise

The three friends kept moving as fast as they could
for as long as they could. They focused so strongly
on getting as far away as possible from Duck's
Village that they didn't hear the Song rising and
rising behind them. After a long and anxious time,
when the Sun was beginning to go down, they
stopped to rest by a sparkling stream of clear
water. The Boy and Coyote jumped in, splashing
each other and laughing loudly in relief. Owl
groomed herself while perched on a rock. She was
silent, but she was relieved as well. The splashing
and laughing began to wind down, and while Owl
prepared to hunt and soar in big loops and circles
through the night sky, the Boy and Coyote lay
down, falling deeply asleep almost immediately.

When Owl returned and the two friends awoke,
nobody talked about what had happened. It was
just too awful to talk about, so there was a silent
agreement not to speak of it.

Not speaking of important things puts a burden on
the heart. As the days went on, all three travellers
found themselves jumping at shadows, startled by
sudden noises, and tossing and turning through the
night (or, in Owl's case, the day) instead of sleeping
deeply and fully. They didn't know what was wrong,

they just knew that something was wrong. And they didn't know what to do about it.

The landscape began to change. The Boy, Coyote, and Owl could smell something in the air - a scent like water, but deeper and different. They were curious to see what was coming - but they were also afraid. Fear is even heavier than sadness, and the fear was eating into them like a worm inside a tomato, from the inside out.

One night while the Boy and Coyote were tossing and turning, Owl flew up and up and up. The Moon was bright, and the world was the mysterious cool blue color day folks rarely get to see. Owl didn't talk much, but she saw pretty much everything. As she hovered high up in the sky, something caught her eye - it looked like a long silver ribbon of water. It was the biggest thing Owl had ever seen. It was so big that Owl could not see the ending of it, and it was right in line with their travelling.

Owl did not know if she was full of joy, afraid, or awed right to her bones by this, so she continued to hover. What happened then is what happens when something that Mother Earth created is so big that it pushes us hard and heals us inside. Owl felt her rapidly beating bird's heart break. She felt all of the awful memories of Duck's Village surface. Sure flyer that she was, she almost fell out of the sky. Her heart breaking freed her heart, as she finally looked bravely at what had happened. She realized how much she loved her friends, and how fragile they were - her friend the Boy could have easily died. She didn't want to think of a world without the Boy and Coyote, but she knew it could happen. She knew that loving them was a fearsome thing with loss around every turn, but she couldn't imagine not loving them.

 With that thought, Owl became wise.

She dropped downwards through the sky, looking like a silver arrow flying surely to the target. She dropped right on top of her friend Coyote, hooting in his ear, "Wake up! Wake up! I have something to tell you!". She messed up the Boy's already messy hair, "Wake up! Wake up! This is important!"

Well, you can imagine how startled the Boy and Coyote were. They jumped up in a panic, and began to run away. Owl hooted again, "No, stop! You're safe! You're safe! I have to tell you something, we have to talk! I love my friends, and we must talk!"

The Boy and Coyote turned back. They looked at Owl just glowing in the night with love for her two friends. It was hard to look at her, but she was so beautiful. The Boy's heart broke open, and he just thumped down onto the ground and began to cry. He owned a very simple heart, so it was one that was easy to fix. He felt the fragility and the iron strength of love. His face was wet, shining in the moonlight. He felt the heavy burden of memory begin to lift.

On the other hand, Coyote's heart was a patchwork quilt full of mends and awkward stitches. That made it well-repaired and very strong. But it had been broken so hard and so many times that it was complicated to fix. He didn't want his heart to break yet again, because every time your heart breaks, it becomes harder and harder to fix it. He began to howl. It was a painful howling, and his voice cracked with grief many times. He couldn't stand it, yet he couldn't help it. He had to love his friends, he had to fix his poor heart one more time, and maybe many more times. So he did what Coyotes do, and he Howled.

The Boy and Owl listened silently with all of their attention. They moved towards Coyote until he was enveloped in loving arms and wings. Owl and the Boy held their friend for hours while the night got deeper and deeper.

Coyote finally got all howled out. His heart broke open and healed yet again. He was kind of embarrassed by all this emotion, and he hid his head in the Boy's skinny chest. "I'm sorry." he muttered. "I should have just kept my big mouth shut. I always talk too much, and now I have messed up my friendships. You must think I'm as weak as a newborn Pup." The Boy and Owl were surprised to hear this. They thought Coyote was stronger than either of them, and they said so. It takes strength to turn things into a Joke - that's the big secret of Clan Coyote. So they just hugged Coyote some more. The Boy found Coyote's best ticklish spots deciding that a good tickling match was exactly what was needed.

Comes out, that was good medicine. You can't laugh and be ashamed at the same time. Coyote got himself back to being himself, and he and the Boy sat on the ground chuckling and tired wiping happy tears and sad tears off their faces. All three friends looked at each other with eyes that were brighter than they had been lately, and certainly with hearts that were healed and much lighter.

Owl sighed deeply and began to speak. "My friends," she began, "I'm so happy we have lifted this heaviness from our hearts. I'm so happy I have such wonderful friends. And I have something huge to tell you." She stopped dramatically (Owl can be a bit of a jokester, too sometimes. And Owl was really enjoying this moment.).

"Well? What is it?" said the Boy.

"Geezelouise!" yipped Coyote,"The suspense is just killing me! Please tell us!"

Owl smiled a tiny and mysterious smile while looking truly Owlish. Slowly she said, "I've seen the Rim of the World, and we are very close."

14. Corazon Chooses to Rise

In the Village that used to Duck's, the People were feeling lost. A few of them still believed in Duck and his talk of selfishness and hate. They were finally told that they could choose to leave, or they could choose to live and rebuild their Village in hope and love for all. There was some grumbling, one or two People decided to leave, and that was it. While the Village had brought back the Traders, the crops were growing, the water was clean again, the People felt like they were drifting along. They wanted more. They wanted to be more than just walking along from day to day.

Corazon saw all of this. Like Owl, Corazon watched much and spoke seldom. And then only when she had something to say, not to just chatter away the time. She decided to hold a meeting. The People were curious as to why someone as reticent as Corazon would hold a meeting, so of course everyone came.

Because she traveled to many Villages in her work as a healer, Corazon saw a lot of things. One of the things that truly talked to her heart were the Children like the Boy. Each child was very different, yet each Child could be healed in some way. She was adept at seeing what shape that healing should take, and many families were the happier for her intervention. She had a dream about a Village where these Children could live and grow - and be loved on their journey. So she spoke about her dream. In very simple words she outlined how her Village could become this place.

The People listened. Because it was so unlike Duck and his hate, some People found it hard to hear. What? Take care of other People's Children? Love them? Help them to reach the fullness of who they could be? While it did not sit well with them in their stunted hearts, they slowly began to see an economic advantage to her plan. If these Children grew strong and healthy on their own unique path, that could only benefit the Village. Other People felt their hearts just grow and blossom listening to Corazon's vision.

At the end of her talking, Corazon humbly thanked her People for listening, and turned to go. Someone in the crowd yelled "Stop! Don't go! Listen to us!" She turned, and the People as one began to cheer and clap and stomp. Soon they were dancing. Someone picked her up and twirled her around. A mother with a small Child gave her a hug and a kiss, whispering to her that she knew her Child was one of the different ones, and she would welcome Corazon's vision for the Village and her Child. This went on and on until Corazon was happy, but very tired. The oldest Person in the Village came forward and looked into her eyes. "Corazon," the person said, "Your vision of our Village is a good one. As the oldest here, I say so be it! Blessed be! We feel you need to be our new leader - you have shown both heart and courage. Will you accept?"

Coarzon didn't know what to do. She was thrilled and scared all at the same time. Finally, happy tears came. Through her tears, she accepted.

And so the work began.

15. Duck, Redux

Duck wandered in circles naked and alone. His tiny feet hurt. His skin hurt. What was left of his mind hurt. Sometimes People saw him on the outskirts of the Village, and while they were no longer afraid of him, they really did not wish to interact with him. They left out food for him, which he greedily ate, but that was it. The People decided to let Mother Earth deal out Her own justice on him.

Duck had built a persona of himself as an absolute authority. He had challenged all Creation to bow before him. When that view broke apart, his consciousness, his awareness of self went completely blank. In other words, the person that had been Duck, and all of his history had been destroyed. What was left was simply a body wandering around.

His wandering became a pattern around the edge of the Village. People pretty much knew when to expect him, and were no longer frightened by his presence. One morning when Duck awoke he felt something different in the air. He felt a pull to move deeper and deeper into the woods. Walking along, he heard birds singing, he heard water moving, he heard the sound of the wind in the trees. These were all things we take for granted - but Duck had never had the ears to hear, being so wrapped up in his own story.

He noticed a red cardinal perching ahead of him, and he mindlessly began to follow the bright color through the deepening forest.

The small bright bird was moving with purpose and plan. Pulling Duck deeper and deeper into the forest. Duck came to a clearing, and the bright bird flew up into the sky. Duck watched it go, then just stood there. Because he did not know what to do next.

He heard a low and even voice. "Hello, Duck. Here you are. After all of your scheming and shouting, and creation of sadness, here you are." Duck stared blankly around. He had never heard such a voice, and something in him woke up a little.

The Woman sat in the clearing. There were no Wolves with her. She looked older, tireder, the flowers in her hair were faded, and there was grief in her voice. "Duck, how could you respect Mother Earth when you had no mother yourself? How could you not be a monster? Everyone told you that you were a monster, and so you became one. How could you not be filled with hate, when every face you saw hated yours? Come over here and sit awhile, Duck. Come over here."

No one had ever spoken to Duck like this, and a tiny, still sentient part of his mind responded. He limped over, and sat down heavily.

The Woman began to sing. She sang about mothers who love their children. Wolf-mothers, Deer-mothers, Bird-mothers, all mothers everywhere. She sang her sadness that Duck had never known what it was like for his Mother to pick him up, hug and kiss him, and tuck him safely into sleep. She sang that Duck was tired, and that it was time to sleep safely in the arms of Mother Earth.

As she sang, Duck seemed to become younger and younger. His body yielded to Mother Earth. A smile, probably his first, snuck silently onto his face. Finally, the song ended. Duck sighed a deeply contented sigh, put his thumb firmly into his mouth, and curled up on the fragrant and cool pine needles falling deeply and happily asleep for the only time in his life.

The Woman stood, stretching out her back. It cracked, and she sighed. This had been hard work, and not joyful work. She was glad it was done. She laid a blanket over Duck, then like his mother would have done long ago, placed a kiss on his forehead. She called her Wolves to her from where they had been waiting deep in the forest, and headed back

to her garden. Her heart was heavy, but her spirit
felt that balance had been restored.

Duck slept on and on, held fast and safely by
Mother Earth. Some People say he woke up and
became a Healer in a place far away. Others say
he sleeps still. Nobody really knows, but no one in
the Village ever saw him again. Every now and
then a red bird would perch nearby, wherever he
was- fixing a bright bead of an eye on him, then
flying away up into the sky.

16. How to Turn at the Rim of the World

Owl flew high into the sky every night, just for the
pleasure of looking at the ever-larger bright silver
stream. It was immense, almost terrifying to look at,
and yet it was soothing as well. The longer Owl
looked, the more she grew into her wisdom and her
Clan Owl heritage.

Back on the ground in the early morning, she would
tell the Boy and Coyote what she had seen. They
were all filled with wonder, yet the question
remained - which way were they going to turn when
they reached the Rim of the World? They debated
and debated. The talk just went around in circles
with no solution. One morning, after yet another
endless discussion Owl said, "I have an idea. What
if we just let it go, and trust ourselves to know what

to do when the time comes?" she went on, "I am thinking sometimes, that when we just trust ourselves, we know what to do, and sometimes when we talk and talk, we lose our way. We are very close, let's just wait, and I am thinking we will just know."

Not having a better plan, or any plan at all, the Boy and Coyote breathed a sigh of relief, agreeing with Owl.

And a few days later they stood at the Rim of the World.

While the immensity of the ocean had become familiar and somehow soothing to Owl, the Boy and Coyote were simply overwhelmed. The Boy did not know if he was terrified or filled with joy at the sight of it rolling on and on, seemingly without end. He did not understand the word "awe", but that's what he was feeling. Coyote, for once had absolutely nothing to say. He just looked and looked and looked, grinning hugely with satisfaction that he and his friends had, indeed, gotten to the Rim of the World. They moved gingerly down the beach, and tentatively stuck their toes into the water.

It felt wonderful. Beautifully cool, sand sliding between their toes, standing ankle deep, they watched the Sun go down. The water turned crimson, the sky grew a deep clear blue, and the three felt happy and peaceful. Coyote and the Boy made a camp near the water's edge, enjoying the sweet sound of the waves, while Owl flew off into the evening sky. As she left, she hooted softly back to her two friends, "Sleep easy, I am sure we will have our answer in the morning. Sleep well." She went off to fly for the sheer joy of flying, and the Boy and Coyote curled up, falling asleep quickly and contentedly.

17. Corazon and the Three-Legged Dog

Corazon kept telling herself that she should be happy. After all, Duck was gone, the people in the Village were deeply ashamed of their behavior while under Duck's spell, the Traders had come back, crops were thriving again and all was well. She said this to herself often, and sometimes she almost believed it. But. Sometimes she felt like she was looking at a big empty spot that felt like a question she did not want to look at. She SHOULD be happy, she told herself. She was respected, she had been instrumental in helping to resurrect the crops and getting the Traders to come back to the Village. People came to her all day long because of her good advice and good heart. Wasn't that enough to make anyone happy? Wasn't she being foolish thinking in the darkest time of the night about what she really wanted? Wasn't she being selfish for wanting to see and learn more about the world? She began to cry about the smallest things - good things, sad things, happy things - anything and everything got the tears going. This went on until Corazon began to doubt her heart and her mind. She still did good in the Village, but that hole she did not want to look at just got bigger and bigger until it seemed to be all she could see. She knew she needed to do something, take some action, but she kept telling herself that the People of her Village needed her, and she should not be so selfish as to explore where her own happiness was.

Deep down, where she was afraid to look, Corazon knew why she was unhappy. She was doing the work for other people, but it was not her true work. She wanted to learn more, see more, and do much more than she was doing. So she sort of walked through each day with half of her heart roaming out somewhere, not wanting to come back to her. That's why she was crying - when your heart is out roaming, and you're not connected to what you're doing, you simply cannot hide your sadness. It will find ways to leak out.

She finally needed to have that conversation with her heart, and she went deep into the woods to a clearing that was her secret spot for peace and quiet. She sat with her feet splashing in the fast running stream, trying to face the fact that while what she was doing was good work, it simply was not her work. She felt half there, half here, and it was a while before she became aware of a quiet whimpering and moaning. When she heard it, she jumped up in a heartbeat, angry at herself for being so unaware of a creature in pain. She began to follow the sound, which seemed so small and so helpless. She thought about the terror she had seen on the Boy's face, and heard that terror echoed in the constant whimpers and moans she was hearing. She hoped the Boy was well, wherever he and his companions were, and she sent them a silent blessing.

"Little One!" she called out, "Where are you? Keep making noises! Don't give up! I will find you!" She began to systematically search through the heavy underbrush, as the terrified sounds continued. She moved slowly and with purpose, missing nothing.

What she found hurt her heart, and yet pulled it back together in a whole. She saw a young Pup, not Wolf, not Coyote, but Clan Dog panting and moaning in pain. A youngster, with a deep furry black and white coat, little triangle ears, and the bluest eyes Corazon had ever seen.

The Pup was also the most injured animal she had ever seen still living. Some careless Trapper had forgotten a baited trap after leaving with their ill-gotten gain. One of the Pup's front legs lay crushed hopelessly in the trap. It was obvious that she had been wandering for quite some time, her coat was dirty and matted, and her bright eyes were dull from dehydration. Corazon saw that the Pup's gums were white and she was panting heavily. As a Healer, she knew that there was not much time to save the Pup. She moved in quickly, pulling bandages and herbs out from the pack she always carried. She also pulled out her knife and said a healing prayer for the Pup, while angrily cursing the greedy and thoughtless Trappers. She held the Pup tightly, gave her a kiss on the top of her furry head for luck, took a deep breath, and removed the crushed leg from the weary little body.

The Pup passed out with an almost grateful sigh. Corazon swiftly carried her back to the stream, washing the wound in the quickly running water. Then she packed it with herbs, wrapping it tightly with a clean bandage. She sat by the stream for a long time holding the Pup, hoping she would survive.

She did. She lay quiet, barely breathing for a long time, but Corazon could feel her heart beating with increasing strength each passing hour. She moved slowly and cautiously carrying the Pup as she made her way back to the Village.

When she walked into the Village, she was predictably bombarded with requests, complaints, worries and wants. For the first time in her life, she simply walked through the crowd, not attending to them, focusing on the Pup in her arms fighting for life. Corazon could feel her bright, loving spirit, and was determined that she live. What she was going to do with a three-legged dog in her life was anyone's guess, but Corazon knew magic when she saw it.

The Pup, being very young, healed quickly and well. She was just fine with three legs, and moved as surely and swiftly as any Dog Corazon had

seen. The Pup's eyes were the brightest blue that a
winter sky offers on the coldest day of the year, so
Corazon named her Sky. That was a good name,
and Sky chose to take it for her own.

Sky and Corazon spent many hours in their quiet
spot in the woods by the clear running stream.
Unlike the Boy, Corazon did not know how to speak
animal language, so she puzzled about
communicating with Sky. Sky, on the other hand,
being Clan Dog, was born knowing how to speak
fluent People. Slowly, Corazon began to be able to
understand Sky.

Clan Dog's language is delightful. It can have all
the deep wisdom of Clan Wolf, all the bad jokes of
Clan Coyote, and all the love for People that is
unique to Clan Dog. Through learning this
language of depth, humor and love, Corazon
became more aware of her true purpose and she
began to see what she needed to do.

18. The Boy and Coyote Get to Play

Sometimes life is so serious that all we can look at
is getting through the day. Sometimes just putting
one foot in front of the other is all we can do. Yet all
beings need to play, explore, see shapes in the
clouds, and maybe tell a long and rambling story
with no point other than telling a long and rambling
story. The Boy and Coyote were certainly no
exceptions to this. Owl had plenty of play time
diving and swooping through the night sky, but the
Boy and Coyote had not. They felt it as a dull pain
at the back of their necks, a heaviness in their
bodies, and sighs that seemed to come all the way
up from their toes. While the Earth still seemed full
of wonder, things appeared to be a little bit gray
around the edges. They did not realize this, but Owl
saw it. She flew back to them early one morning,
and decided to talk with them. She told them what
she was seeing, and how difficult it was to watch
her friends pushing so hard to reach their goal.

They were at a place where they could rest, she
said. Besides, they had not yet felt a real pull about
which way to turn -and that uncertainty told her that
they were not ready to resume their journey. She
would patrol the night, keeping them safe, and they
should have some time to explore and learn about
this timeless spot at the rim of the World. Both of
them fought the idea, wanting to push on. Coyote
sat up tall, turning his face away from Owl, while

the Boy simply sat cross-legged, folded his limber body up, and stuck his face right into the sand. He even spit a few times, just to try and add what he felt to be subtle commentary. Both were convinced that they were doing a truly excellent job of ignoring Owl until they heard what can only be described as hoots that sounded quite a bit like the Owl version of riotous laughter.

Coyote turned his head and squinted up his eyes. The Boy peered up a little bit, one eye peeking through the wet sand. Owl continued to laugh. Finally, wiping her moonlike eyes with a wingtip, she began to speak to her friends.

"Dear Boy, and dear Coyote, we have been through a journey that has tested us, and we have come to a place we did not even know existed until now. I can watch the trails through the night while I soar and hunt, and I will make sure you remain safe. Why not take some time and explore the Rim of the World? Think of the stories you could tell.". Well, that part got Coyote's attention, and he cocked his head, considering. "Think of how much fun you could have exploring this place!" At this, the Boy sat up and looked at Owl with something that was almost a smile, sand crusting on his upturned sunburned nose. Finally, both of them agreed to Owl's wisdom. Sighing happily, Owl found a perch, and fell peacefully asleep. It was good to be wise, she thought, and even better to be listened to.

19. An Interlude. A Breather. Play.

True to her word, Owl patrolled the night sky focusing on the trail the Traders had created from a long-ago deer track. The three travelers had moved parallel to this trail on their journey to the Rim of the World. The Boy and Coyote slept easily knowing that Owl was always watching.

Their days were spent exploring, swimming, climbing up the rocky cliffs, as well as lazily telling tall tales and bad jokes. In short, it was exactly what the Boy, who did not know how to play, needed. When we play, we show our true selves. The Boy was delighted by playing, and was enjoying this respite enormously. For his part, Coyote was running and leaping, and putting the past where it belonged.

They discovered the tide pools along the coast, and marveled at the sea creatures they found. The pools were little universes containing wonders that changed daily. The Boy would find the tallest tree he could find, climb up it, and try to see where the endless shining ribbon of water ended. He found it fantastic and unbelievable that the water seemed to go on forever. He loved thinking of how vast the water was, yet how the tide pools were tiny and contained a whole world. His mind was growing

and expanding and learning new concepts
constantly - that's what play does.

20. Sky and Corazon

Despite the fact that Sky was missing a leg she was agile, strong, and quick. Corazon made sure to push her to her full potential and Sky responded by becoming a true companion and partner. Having never had a working relationship with a dog before, Corazon was awed by how Sky seemed to read her every emotion, and how willing she was to work. Sky became Corazon's co-worker, carrying her supplies in a pack Corazon created for her.

So they travelled North and South along the great river the Villages were clustered along, and Eastward along the Trader's path that was once a deerpath. Corazon tended to her own People as a leader and an organizer, and to many others as well. She had always taken great joy in being a Healer, and she was trying hard to convince herself that she was irreplaceable. In the evenings she and Sky sat and watched the Sun go to sleep in the West, and she wondered what was past the great river she had always lived alongside.

Sky was trying hard to communicate, but it was slow going. Corazon had spent most of her life working with People. Clan Dog's speech was not familiar to her, and her logical mind fought this while her imagination reveled in it.

What Sky saw was that Corazon was getting more and more used up. Sometimes, people who are Healers don't see when they need healing. They just keep going. Because there are so many needing help and healing that most Healers will feel that they are being lazy if they stop to take care of themselves. Corazon was keeping up, but Sky saw how weary she was. She was forgetting where she put things,and she was waking up during the night thinking it was time to get up and get going. She saw that Corazon was eating, but not enjoying her food. She saw that Corazon was looking right at her friend, Sky, but not really seeing her. Sky had no idea what she could do to help her partner and friend, so she watched and listened, and hoped Corazon would figure out what she needed to do.

Corazon loved working with the Different Children. Each child was a unique puzzle just waiting to be solved. She put a lot of her time and love into reaching out to these families. So many of these children had so much to give once some of the keys to their puzzle were discovered. It was challenging to find the right clues, but so wonderful to see the whole Child begin to have a voice and a place in the world. She was working with a Child one day, and delighting in the clear and piping singing voice she was hearing, as well as the brightest smile she had seen in a long time. She called out to the Child's parents, her face clearly showing her happiness and delight. "Listen!" she said, "Do you hear that voice? The words are so clear, and the melody is lovely!" she laughed, full of joy, and said "Look at that smile! Isn't that just the happiest smile you've ever seen?"

She heard nothing back, and turned to see both parents in a long discussion about what to buy from the Traders when they next arrived. The father caught her glance and said, "Oh, well, singing is nice and all. I guess. What about learning how to plow the fields - or even taking care of the chickens? What good is singing?" The mother then said, "I work hard and I see no reason to smile. Our Child should be grateful, and learning how to work. Who cares about smiling? I liked it better when there were no smiles. At least I wasn't reminded of how hard I work so other people can sing and smile." Then they turned back to their conversation, ignoring Corazon.

Corazon hugged the Child, and whispered into a sweetly curving little ear, "Keep smiling, keep singing, Little One. We need your magic. Please don't let anyone take it away from you."

Standing up to leave, Corazon became aware of an uncomfortable, tight feeling in her throat - as if she had swallowed a hot rock. She felt a heaviness in her heart - as if she were floating in cold water with no land in sight. Her eyes were dry and hurting - as if she had looked at the Sun. She politely said her farewell, and began walking away. She heard a voice behind her saying,"Next time, teach something useful. We don't need to feed another mouth, especially one that only has singing and smiling to offer!" She did not turn to respond, and began to move more quickly.

She started to run, feeling her bare feet pounding on the earth, moving faster and faster. The feeling in her throat became stronger, and hurt more and more as she moved. She didn't think or care where she was going, she just kept moving. Sky was puzzled at her friend's strange behavior, but kept right at her side, even though she was pretty sure Corazon did not even know she was there.

When we hurt, we often run to the places where we feel safe and comforted. No different with Corazon. She found herself in her forest clearing with the bubbling stream. She sat down and splashed her face with cool water. She stuck her feet into the stream. She took a deep and shaking breath.

Then the tears came. Corazon didn't even know exactly why she was crying. It just seemed like months and months of giving and watching and trying to make things better for all seemed worthless. She was only one person, she thought, and she could do so little. She thought about the Child's parents, and how they had looked at their Child. A look that said the Child was less than human, less than loveable, less than wonderful. That made her cry even harder, so hard she wasn't aware of Sky snuggling up to her.

Sky was doing her very best to help. She had never seen a Person appear to explode like this, all gasping breaths and tears and snot, and she was worried. She whined a little bit, pushing her round black nose into Corazon's wet face. Corazon dug her fingers into Sky's thick coat, crying and crying. Sky sighed. She didn't know what was wrong with Corazon, but she would wait it out.

21. Looking Upwards

Corazon started talking out loud, trying to find a solution. "I could talk with the parents about what I see!" she said, snuggling her face into Sky's wet fur, "I could tell them how special their Child is, I could talk about potential. I could talk about all sorts of things, I know I could find the right words! I know I could change their hearts!"

From somewhere nearby, cold chirping words came. "Don't bet on it, chica. I wasn't planning on meeting you personally like this but, inconveniently enough, here I am."

Corazon was startled and looked around her. Sky growled, seeing a large not-wolf not-dog laying at the edge of the clearing. Storm leveled his gaze on Sky, and she went quiet.

"Please, stop looking at the ground. Corazon, the answer is rarely housed in the practical, or on the ground. Look up, please." So she looked upwards.

What she saw was familiar on a visceral level, yet alien. She saw a young girl, barely past childhood with oddly chopped scarlet hair, ruthless blue eyes that she wanted to hide from, and lovely translucent skin. Perched far up on a tree limb. While Sky continued to watch Storm, Corazon thought about how to respond. At a loss for words, she finally relied on her manners. "Hello, I don't believe we've met, but I think I know you. Uh, why are you up in a tree, and who is the large not-wolf not-dog looking at Sky? I hope I'm not offending you? Please?"

Redbird gave her snorty laugh. "Corazon, I'm beyond offense, and yes, you know me although not on a face to face level. I'm happy you recognize that." She then began to hum the Song of Ale and Mead.

Corazon finally smiled. "That was YOU?" she almost laughed. "That was amazing! How dld you do that?"

Redbird dropped easily to the ground. "I have no idea." she said. "It needed to be done, so I just did it. A lot of my life is like that." she gave Corazon a shy and crooked smile,"But Corazon, it's all about you right now. And Storm is no threat, he's simply my travelling companion." At this, Storm grumbled agreement and curled up in a large and loose ball, falling quickly asleep in the way only Dogs and young Children can. Sky sighed in obvious great relief. She hopped a little closer to Corazon, looking at this stranger with curiosity.

22. Coyote Remembers How to Remember

While he loved his traveling companions, every now and again, Coyote just needed to walk alone for a while. Sometimes the past was just too much on his mind, and the only way he knew to make it go away for a time was to walk, trot, and run until he just wore himself out. This was one of those days. He told the Boy he was going to go and walk. The Boy simply hugged his friend, and said he would be waiting.

So Coyote trotted off aimlessly. The more he tried to not remember his pack, the more he remembered them. This dark remembering weighed so much that his walking got slower and slower and his sighs got deeper and deeper. He was so far away from what was around him that he almost crashed into the very Large Golden and Silver Wolves standing silently right in front of him.

Coyote jumped. "You two again?" he barked. Then he thought better of that comment. "I mean, uh, greetings noble Wolves- what brings your company to this humble Coyote? Sorry, but you startled me." Then he brightened up. "Is your Person with you? It would be wonderful to see her again. Is she here, too? Not that I don't enjoy your presence, of course…oh, bother, I just never say the right thing to you guys."

The two Wolves exchanged a glance, "Shall we tell him?" said the Golden Wolf, "Shall we?"

"No", replied the Silver Wolf, "I think it should be a surprise!" He then turned to Coyote, "Come with us, let's run and we will show you."

Coyote was actually rather pleased that these two had shown up and he put his self-absorbed reverie behind him. "I'm ready, I'm ready!" he yipped, "Let's GO!"

So they ran, swiftly and silently In the lovely flowing way canids run - looking like joyful water. Finally, they came to a quiet cove along the beach. Coyote looked eagerly, hoping to see his friend, The Woman. And then to his immense joy, there she was standing tall with new flowers in her hair and a warm smile greeting him. He forgot what little dignity he naturally owned, and just threw himself into her arms, licking her face in happy greeting. "It's YOU!" he barked "It's YOU!"

After a time, they both sat down and looked at each other. Both sighed a happy and contented sigh. The Woman ruffled the hair on Coyote's head, and scratched behind his ears. "Hello, old friend." she smiled, "It is so good to see you again. I knew our paths would cross, but I didn't know when." Coyote began to breathlessly tell her all of the adventures they had experienced, and she laughed, making a shooing motion with her hands. "I know all about that stuff" she said, "I know. And you were very brave and very smart."

"I was?" Coyote was amazed (as well as a little bit pleased and proud she would say that). "Well, I suppose I was, then."

She looked at him in a way that was taking measure and loving at the same time. Coyote wanted to get all squirmy and uncomfortable, but he didn't. He knew he was better than that, so he gently returned her gaze. Finally, she nodded. "Friend, I need your help." she sighed. "I think this is something you need, and we" she indicated to the Wolves, "need your help. Look over here, please." she walked over to a basket, and Coyote looked inside.

He saw a very surprised pair of blue eyes, a pointy little nose, and two amazingly huge ears picking up every sound. It was a fuzzy little baby Coyote. The last sad, cold and frozen part of his heart melted, just like that.

"A baby?" he yipped, jumping up and down with excitement "You brought me a baby? I love him already, but why is he here, where is his Pack?" Then he stopped and looked at the Woman, understanding. He spoke with determination, "Well, if anyone can bring up a pup, it's me. You picked the right guy, that's for sure - look at how I'm bringing up the Boy! What is his name?" he asked, peering into the basket with eagerness and joy.

"We call him Little Brother, or Nika for short." the Woman replied. His story is like yours, but he is too young to take care of himself, so we thought of you. Will you accept him as your pup in Clan Coyote?"

Of course, Coyote did not even think twice about it. "Well, yes! He is tiny, he needs me!"

"And you need him, friend Coyote." sighed the Woman." Remembering is good, it makes room in your heart, but remembering nothing but darkness only leads you to more darkness. Your pack does not want to be remembered for the darkness. They want to be remembered for all the love you shared."

Coyote started washing Little Brother, making sure he was very clean. Little Brother responded by batting at Coyote's nose. "I know you're right. I have needed something to push me ahead for a long time. While I mourn Little Brother's loss, I am happy for our gain. I will teach him, love him and protect him. He is my Pack now." as an afterthought, he added, "And I will teach him every one of the many jokes I know. Especially the burping jokes." He grinned hugely. He knew that the Boy would be overjoyed with Little Brother, and

Owl would get used to him and learn to love him as well.

A smile cascaded across The Woman's face. "Of course" she said simply. "Of course."

23. Little Brother Goes Home

Coyote and the Woman and her Wolves did not say
goodbye. Instead they said, "We will see you
again.", which is what good friends always say to
each other. Coyote set off with Little Brother in tow.
While they had not gone a long distance from
where he was sleeping, Little Brother was truly
little, and needed to rest frequently. Finally Coyote
just slung him up over and onto his back and
moved at a steady trot. Little Brother fell asleep,
and Coyote balanced him easily on his back.

As he had hoped, the Boy was delighted. Little
Brother was kissed and picked up way over the
Boy's head, tickled, belly rubbed, as well as rocked
to sleep. As he slept, Coyote told the story to the
Boy who listened wide eyed.

They both agreed that the world was a far more
magical place than they had known before they
began their journey, and they wondered what
magic would happen when they moved on.

When Owl woke up for the evening, Coyote told the
tale of the arrival of Little Brother again, adding only
a few embellishments like how he easily outran the
Wolves, and how he saved the Woman from
drowning in the big water. Both the Boy and Owl
knew these were made up parts, but being good
friends, they allowed Coyote his story. Little Brother

listened, wide eyed. Given that he had been snoozing in a basket while all of this occurred, it could very well be truth, he thought. Coyote became a bit of a hero to him, and he began to feel like this was home and pack.

Coyote and the Boy had a wonderful time teaching Little Brother about being a pack member, and he was a happy and willing pupil. He remembered very little about what had happened before the Woman found him, save that he had been cold and hungry. Coyote saw that Little Brother did not carry the burden of memories that Coyote carried. Oddly, this made Coyote's burden lighter as he shared Little Brother's joy in learning.

The days rolled on like the waves in the water. The light was becoming more and more golden, and the shadows were getting longer. The nights were sweet-smelling and clear. They knew cooler weather would come, but they still felt no pull towards which direction to move. Owl said that was just fine. We don't always need to have a goal or a destination, there are times when just breathing and living are simply enough.

And that's exactly what they did. Every breath was pleasure, every meal delightful, every joke was funnier than the one before. They discovered that Little Brother was very good at telling jokes - but his jokes were Thinking Jokes. You had to take a minute for the joke to sink in, and then you began laughing. His eyes lost their little baby blueness, beginning to take on a rich golden color. He began to grow into his very large ears, and his baby coat was replaced by a color that reminded Coyote of the Golden Wolf. In fact, Coyote was starting to wonder if Little Brother really was Clan Coyote after all. It would be just like the Woman to do that, he thought. Not to trick Coyote, but to teach him something. He wondered what the lesson could possibly be, and realized that he would know when he knew - that's how lessons work. At the end of the day, when they all snuggled together and Owl began her journey for the night, Coyote really did not care. Little Brother, Owl, and the Boy were his pack and Coyote's heart finally regained a true home.

24. Segue to Somewhere Else

Along the beach a woman was dancing. A large
woman, with midnight dark skin, and eyes
protected by a scarf. Her abundant hair was
wrapped tightly around her head and she was
clothed in loose, easy, and brightly-colored
clothing. She was stomping into the sand. She was
kicking up tiny waves at the shoreline. She leapt
high into the air, and came back down steady and
sure. She was beautiful to watch, and her dance
was one of healing, summoning, and protecting.

25. Practical Corazon Gets Shaken Up and Stirred

She had always prided herself on being a
cool-headed, pragmatic person, but ever since the
Song of Ale and Mead, the Song of Power, and
Duck's subsequent departure, Corazon's life had
changed. Well, she had changed, really. She was
seeing the world around her in a more aware and
magical way - although she wasn't aware of that
yet. What she did know was that she was in a world
of hurt. She had never really paid much attention to
that part of herself, and like many people who run
on their brains, forgetting their heart and intultion,
she was surprised to learn how incredibly deep and
wide this world really is.

For instance. Here she was, sitting in the woods
with a three-legged dog who was trying very hard to
communicate with her, and a young woman who
was apparently some kind of supernatural being.
And then there was that gigantic not-wolf-nor-dog
cooly watching the whole exchange. But she knew
her life needed to change, and she knew it was
time to stop smugly congratulating herself for
remaining dispassionate, because she wasn't that
person anymore. It was time to leap in and move
on.

Corazon and Redbird talked. Redbird talked about
not having a place where she belonged, while
Corazon spoke of being too tied to a Village and

the People who lived there. They both talked about the isolation within the two very different situations. They spoke about how you can help people, but you can't fix them to be what you think they should be.

Finally, they spoke about the magic surrounding the Different Children. One could fix all one wanted with those Children, but the only way they truly grew was when they were offered love and acceptance. While they would always retain their different-ness, loving and enjoying that difference was the key for everyone, Different or not.

During this exchange, Sky was listening intently. While she knew how much Corazon loved her, the woman was pretty deaf when it came to Sky communicating with her. They could communicate little things, like "Stop here.", or "I'm tired.", but that was all. The problem was that Corazon felt like that was all there was. Sky had a lot to say, so this was frustrating to her. It was obvious to Sky that Redbird communicated on all kinds of different levels, and she was hoping that Redbird could help Corazon learn to speak with her.

Then it became time for the conversation to end. Corazon felt more whole than she had felt in a long time. She knew what she needed to do, and she acknowledged her pull to where the Sun went down at night. She had learned that loneliness comes wrapped into all sorts of different packages, and

Redbird's story had shown her that even powerful beings could feel that ache. Corazon was no longer looking at Redbird with awe and some fear, she was seeing Redbird as a friend, albeit a rather supernatural one. Redbird picked up on the thought, laughed a little and said, "Thank you, Corazon. Thank you very much. I have another friend among People. You met him when I sang the Song of Ale and Mead." at this, Corazon clapped her hands in excitement. "Oh! He was so special! I think he must be wise! But he was so little and so scared - and it was so hard to just let him go off with a Coyote and an Owl. Do you know where he is? Is he alright?" Redbird shook her head. "I can tell you he is doing well, but it would disturb the pattern too much to tell you more. Sometimes people we know only for a breath or two change us the most. So, take that and run with it, chica. Time for you to have your own adventures."

Corazon stood to go. Sky looked intently at Redbird. Redbird looked back at Sky with her clear gaze. "One more thing, Corazon. Listen to Sky. She is trying so hard to speak with you. She will help you on this journey." Before Corazon could answer, Redbird was gone, just like that, and Storm, large as he was, was gone as well.

26. Corazon Becomes a Wanderer

Corazon did not waste any time. Her mind was made up and she was ready to go. She spoke with the Elders and the Midwives, leaving her duties in capable hands. Feeling both humbled and liberated that she could be so easily replaced, she packed up her things, took a deep breath, and left the Village.

Truth be told, she was more excited than apprehensive. While her life so far had been interesting and meaningful, it had also taken place on a very small stage. So heading out in an unknown direction felt just right. She decided to move a bit into the woods, walking alongside the Trader's well-worn path. Sometimes, when she felt like she wanted company she would join them, and sometimes she enjoyed her solitude in the woods. Sky hopped along steadily and happily, enjoying seeing Corazon become at peace with herself. Sky was still frustrated that Corazon wasn't talking with her beyond basic words but she was optimistic that she had taken Redbird's advice to heart.

27. Snake, Sky, and Rose.

Clan Dog has walked beside People for generations. While they can be wise, like Clan Wolf, or jokesters like their Coyote cousins, they are unique because of their bond with People. Sky was no exception, and she loved Corazon with the kind of heart only Clan Dog offers. Corazon, on the other hand, loved Sky but did not see her as a full being in her own right. Sky found this confusing because of Corazon's passionate work with the Different children. She spoke to them just fine, but was deaf to Sky. While they walked, Sky thought about that, always coming to the same conclusion - Corazon just could not hear her. Not just her, Corazon, lovely and loving as she was, seemed deaf to the speech of the trees, the water, the living rocks, as well as the Animal kingdom. While Sky's experience with People was limited, she suspected that most of them were like that - deaf to Creation rolling on all around them. She watched the Traders, and often went to speak with their Horses and Donkeys, who said the same thing. Some People could hear them, but most did not. To Sky, this seemed to be a big flaw in the pattern, and she wondered why Mother Earth had allowed this to occur.

So they walked. Corazon sometimes gathered healing plants, and kept her bag full. They often joined the Traders, who were appreciative of her healing skills. Corazon kept her mind still, allowing her journey to be one of discovery and introspection. The Traders had many stories of different Villages, and Corazon found herself filled with a desire to visit all of them, learning from every journey.

The day had started out with a cold, spitting rain that caused conversation to slow to necessities. The land here was wilder, and Villages few and far between. As they hunkered down to try and cook an evening meal, a traveling woman caught up with them, joining the group. She had hair the color of a ripe eggplant, skin that was tanned from much time spent outside, and a large rangy frame that could be either pretty invisible - or right in your face. She seemed to move in total silence, often surprising others. But her most remarkable feature was her very large, slightly bulging eyes that appeared to watch everything at once. She told the group that her name was Snake because she was a great shaman who transformed others and knew almost everything. While some of the Traders believed her, and Corazon found her interesting, none of the Animals would have anything to do with her. The Horses and Donkeys would shy away from her, rolling their eyes and baring their teeth. Sky would hide behind Corazon, not liking her staring at everyone and everything as if she wanted to take it all apart and consume it in one big gulp. In short, the Animals knew she was up to no good, although the People did not see that.

Snake enjoyed telling anyone who would listen about her accomplishments. Along with her ability as someone who could talk to animals, she also said she was truly magical in working with the Different children, claiming that she could magically cast out the demons she said were afflicting these children. Corazon was always eager to learn more, so she listened to what Snake had to say.

Snake was bothered that Sky hid behind Corazon when she was around. She felt that the Animal kingdom should listen to her. After all, she could communicate with them. What she didn't understand was that while she did communicate with them, they did not like what she had to say. She told the Animals they must obey her, not understanding that when Animals truly obey it is out of love and not fear. Obedience without love is slavery.

In many ways, Snake was very smart. She knew how to listen to people without appearing to be eavesdropping. She knew how to catch people in a bad moment and then later use it against them. She knew how to talk about herself without quite lying, but without really being honest. She made her living following the Traders into Villages, then going to work to do her "magic". While she didn't do too much damage - she certainly didn't do a lot of good.

Now and then, travelers like Corazon would join the Traders on their way to somewhere else. Some, like Corazon were not sure about their destination, while others had a clear purpose. One of those with a purpose was a young child named Rose and her family. Rose was one of the Different children, and her family had heard stories of an entire Village that was dedicated to working with children like her. They decided to leave their Village far to the East, where the Sun rose in order to search for it. Rose was like the flower she was named for. She was delicately boned with pink cheeks, brown eyes and curly, curly black hair. Rose did not speak, she babbled what to others seemed to be nonsense. Sometimes she seemed to become frustrated with the inability of others to understand what she felt she was saying so clearly and then she would lay on the ground for hours screaming. This was why her family was searching for a place where she could grow. Oddly, the Animals understood her perfectly - and they certainly understood her frustration at how very deaf People could be. Sky in particular, enjoyed being around Rose. Sky was also frustrated that no matter how hard she tried, Corazon never seemed to hear her. Rose's family was enjoying their journey. Like Corazon, they liked hearing the Traders talk about the different places they had seen, and People they had met. Some of them knew Corazon, and the story of Duck was one that was told many times.

 Rose and her family talked with Corazon about what could be done to help Rose learn how to speak with other People. Corazon was as stuck as they were. Besides offering patience, love, and security she did not really know how to reach Rose either. They talked long into the night about this while Rose slept with her curly little head resting on Sky. The girl and the dog often talked with each other, too - and both of them wanted to be heard as much as others wanted to hear their voices.

On this night, as the embers burnt low and glowing, Snake wandered into their small circle. She had had a rather profitable day selling information she had overheard to other People who wanted to hear it, or didn't want it to be heard. Most People tend to keep it to themselves when they overhear something not meant for their ears, but Snake had discovered it was an excellent way to make a living. Some People would pay for her to tell, while others would pay her to stay silent. She found it a highly satisfying profession, while made-up magic practiced on simple folks looking for an easy path was every bit as lucrative. She was smiling secretly to herself while wearing a concerned face as she silently glided up to the little campfire. She saw some trade coming her way.

"You all look so worried!" She oozed out the words, trying to make them sound sympathetic, but her words sounded so jarringly off that both Rose and Sky woke up from a deliciously sweet sleep. Rose didn't even bother to open her eyes. She felt the same way about Snake that the Animals did, and wanted nothing to do with her. She could not understand how the grown-up People could be so deaf and dumb to Snake. Sky's eyes were bright blue slits, and she was thinking seriously about growling out a strong message to Snake about her displeasure. She knew Corazon would be horrified by her bad manners, but Snake was really getting under her skin.

"Hey!" Said Snake, still looking concerned, but feeling as satisfied as a weasel in the chicken yard, "Really, you all look so serious! Is it about Rose, poor little lost girl! What a burden you carry! She is so very obviously not right at all! Anyone can see that."

She continued, "I can cure her, you know. This laying on the ground screaming stuff is just about getting everyone's attention. I've seen hundreds of children like her get better. I can do a spell the next time she starts with this nonsense, and you'll see, she'll stop throwing fits to get attention." Corazon was about to say something about what she had seen - which was not at all like what Snake was describing, but then she remembered Duck and his angry speeches. She decided to stay quiet and see what she could find out.

Snake went on and on and on. Finally, Rose's parents, who truly treasured their child, agreed. The next time Rose "had a fit", they would allow Snake to do whatever it was she was going to do.

Sky was also listening. She knew Rose really wasn't following the grownup conversation, as most children find the things that interest grownups to be very boring, but Sky understood every word. And there was no way she was going to let Snake near Rose. She squinted up her eyes even more and lifted a lip to show very white and sharp teeth. With a quick sideways glance towards Corazon, she looked right at Snake and did something she had never done to anyone before in her life. She growled.

Corazon was so surprised that she jumped and let out a little yelp. Snake, however, looked right back at Sky and said to Corazon, "Your dog is a problem, Corazon. She's bad to the bone, I can tell. Maybe I should do some magic on her, too. You know I'm communicating with her, and she has no respect for you. You have spoiled her. Animals are like children - they need to show proper respect and fear to grownups." Again, Corazon was reminded unhappily of Duck. She felt sad for the

Earth that the Mother had more than one Person like Duck crawling around.

Snake and Sky did a stare down for what seemed to be a very long time as Corazon watched uneasily. Finally, Snake looked away, glared at Corazon and slunk off. Sky looked at Corazon, expecting a strong rebuke, and was surprised to see that she was weeping.

"Sky, I'm so wrong about everything." she said quietly. "I call myself a healer, and yet I feel that all I know is potions. This world is such a wonderful place, and there is just so much to learn. And I don't feel like I'm learning." She sat down on the ground next to Sky and took a shaky breath. "Well, I guess knowing what I don't know is a place to start." Sky, being a Dog, gave Corazon a comforting lick. She was still stung by Snake's words, and did not want Corazon to take them to heart.

Learning isn't always taking a class or reading a book. Many times learning is simply allowing the busy, rational thinking, planning part of the mind to take a rest from trying to manipulate the present, worry about the future, and berate ourselves about the past. Sometimes, we have to let go and allow Spirit to show us what we need. This isn't easy, because we tend to feel that we know better than Spirit. When we feel like that, Spirit will most certainly find a way to humble us. That's what was happening with Corazon. She had felt that people were basically good, some more good than others. That all changed with Duck. She had thought long and hard about how the entire Village had so quickly and thoroughly leapt into his hatred and intolerance. She thought about what Snake had said about Children and the Animal kingdom, and she felt herself sinking into a deep sense of helplessness. Her world had been very small for her entire life. Now it was expanding, and she wasn't sure she liked what she saw.

Redbird had instructed her to listen to Sky. Corazon loved Sky, but she had never before known having a companion from Clan Dog. She was at a loss, so she decided to slow down how busy her mind was, and how sad her heart was, "Watch and learn." She thought to herself, "I think Redbird would tell me to stop talking inside my head, and start watching and listening."

She wiped the tears off her face, gave Sky a fierce little hug and said "Well, Sky, I am going to watch you and learn. It's time for me to get myself right with you." So Sky, being Clan Dog, did what all dogs do when they are delighted with their People. She jumped up on Corazon with a tail waving like a tree in a windstorm, licking her face in pure joy. She almost knocked Corazon down, but she caught herself, returning Sky's enthusiastic hug. Sky thought to herself that maybe Corazon would learn to listen to the Animal kingdom - if she could just keep listening.

28. Rose

So the Trader's caravan progressed towards where
the Sun went to sleep. Corazon was spending less
time with the group, and more time walking quietly
in the woods. She felt like she was beginning to
hear things, not with her ears but with her heart and
her other senses. Trees seemed to be very
interesting - they were all interconnected and there
was constant conversation, as well as a knowledge
of places and happenings far away. Some of the
chatter seemed to be about a small group of beings
at the Rim of the World. Corazon wasn't sure, but
she gathered that only one of the group belonged
to Clan People. She thought fleetingly about the
Boy, she knew he obviously conversed with Owl
and Coyote. It could certainly be done, she thought.
She told herself that she would try even harder.

That led her to looking at Rose. Rose and Sky had
a strong bond, and appeared to communicate
freely. Yet Rose refused the speech of People.
Maybe there was more going on with Rose than
incoherent and scrambled thinking. Maybe there
was a way to communicate with her and Sky.

Corazon was starting to understand how very busy
her mind was, and seeing how that cut her off from
a deeper experience. She was glad she had
chosen to go on this journey instead of staying in
her known and safe world. Sky was sensing this

shift in Corazon's way of being in the world, and was interested to see where it would lead.

The little group of Traders, Snake, Corazon, and Rose's family kept moving towards where the Sun went down. Rose had been very quiet for a very long time, and her family was hoping that this might be a permanent change. But Rose did not feel quiet on the inside - she felt like a storm about to happen. She felt talked at, not listened to. She felt moved around by adults and unable to explore this exciting journey in her own way. She felt that her feelings weren't seen as important - well, she felt that she wasn't important at all. All the adults, she thought, only wanted to make her more like them. In short, Rose did not feel she was allowed to be Rose.

Finally, one day, Rose's storm broke. One more grown up trying to get her to talk to them. They were speaking to her in silly baby talk, not understanding that she understood every word spoken, she simply felt no need to speak to people. She just could not listen to it for another second, so she threw herself down onto the ground and started yelling, kicking and hitting and slapping at anyone who came near her. That was where Snake saw her opportunity and slunk over to Rose's worried parents. "Well, well." she almost chortled, "Looks like your precious Rose is having quite the temper tantrum." Rose's parents looked sadly at Snake. While they didn't like her (it was difficult to impossible to like Snake. She was always right, and she always talked to others as if they were very stupid), maybe she had some kind of solution. "You see," Snake continued, "Rose is simply trying to get you to do what she wants. All of the Different children are like that. They need so much attention, then they get attention, and they throw a fit every time something doesn't go their way. Rose needs to respond to commands, right now she's like a little demon, and she needs someone to talk some sense into her! Watch me…" and before Rose's parents could say anything Snake ran right up to Rose. At this point, Rose was red faced, streaming tears and snot, and getting angier by the second. Snake was the very last grown up she wanted to see, that was for sure. So she leapt up, screamed louder, and promptly punched Snake right in her rather ample belly. This enraged Snake, who truly did think that children should always be docile and humble. Snake started yelling back, barking out orders. "Stop that! Stop it now! Stop! Stop! Stop!" Snake made herself look as threatening as possible, and stood over Rose, who had flopped back down onto the ground. Rose responded by screaming even more loudly, writhing around on the ground as if she were on fire. In a way, she was. She had just had enough of being treated like a non-person, and she was not about to let this bulging-eyed grown up with purple hair stop her.

Snake tried to pick her up, but Rose just slipped to the ground again. Over and over, Rose screaming and Snake yelling out orders. People stopped what they were doing and came to watch. It was a hot day, and pretty soon, they were both covered in dirt and sweat. Snake yelled commands, Rose screamed back, kicked back, slapped back. Nobody knew what to do, and secretly, some folks were interested in seeing this little girl best Snake.

Corazon and Sky ran over, too. While Corazon had seen this behavior with the Different children more than once, she had never witnessed this level of intensity. She was worried that Rose would get hurt, and worried that Snake would hurt her by constantly grabbing her arms and trying to pull her to her feet. She was just about to step in and try to speak calmly to Snake (who was getting more and more out of control with Rose's apparent lack of respect for her prowess), when Sky rushed past her. Sky ran up to Snake and did not hesitate. She jumped in between the two, knocking Snake right down on her rear. Then she went and stood over Rose, nudging her gently, and licking her dirty face, snot and all.

Snake did not go down lightly because she was a rather large woman, and the breath was knocked right out of her. It was quite a while before she could get any words out at all, but when she did, she turned her venom onto Rose and Sky. "Devil dog!" she roared "Evil beast! I don't know why Corazon saved you! She should have let you die in that trap! I don't know why Rose even exists! She's useless! You're both mistakes, you should not even be drawing breath!"

Corazon was rarely moved to anger but by this time she was furious. She moved quickly between the woman and the little girl, and shouted right in Snake's blotched and dirty face, "YOU GO! Don't return! You are nothing more than a false shaman who has only words and no wisdom. YOU GO!" she commanded. Corazon was not a large woman but in this moment she felt as large as a mountain. "YOU GO!"

Amazingly, Snake did just that. She dusted herself off, glared at Corazon and snarled, "You'll see. Someday I will be famous as the person who unlocked the minds of the Different children. You'll see, and you'll wish you were as famous as I will be!" While Corazon highly doubted Snake's rather grand statement, she was relieved to see her moving away as swiftly as she could.

She turned to look at Rose and Sky, and saw them laughing rolling and playing on the ground. They were in perfect harmony with each other, no need for anything as clumsy as words, they were just pure joy and energy. In that moment, Corazon finally understood. Communication is rarely about words. Words are only a frame for energy. Words are only a tiny part of your mind. Corazon stood speechless. She was sensing the communication between Rose and Sky, and it was beautiful beyond words. Her soul was dancing. She sat down on the ground, and reached out her arms. Sky and Rose ran over to her, and the three began crying happy tears, hugging each other hard. Finally, they all calmed down and just sat there in a joyful pile.

After a while Corazon got up and went over to Rose's family. They had watched Snake's performance and their hearts were just breaking. They felt that they must be the worst parents to ever walk the Earth. Corazon understood their thoughts. "No, you are not the worst mother and father to walk this Earth." she said slowly, "Like myself, you just did not know. Rose can learn to talk with you and she can learn to ask for what she needs. She has been communicating all along, we were just too into our need for words to understand. When we come to the next Village, we will find a puppy for Rose to love. This will help to give her a way to learn to communicate. That is the gift of Clan Dog. They are a bridge between our need for words, and true communication from the heart." Rose's parents hugged Corazon, and there were even more happy tears. By this point, Rose and

Sky had found the shade of a large and generous
tree, and were sleeping contentedly.

After that, Snake stayed with the caravan, but she
made sure to put much distance between Rose's
family and Corazon. She could not even look at
Sky. Eventually, Snake found people who would
listen to her babbling about being a great shaman
and she traveled with them - there are always those
people who are so desperate for an answer that
they find someone like Snake. All you have to do is
look around you.

50. A Family Needs a Home

Indeed, the next Village came along quickly. Rose's
family and Coarzon found a litter of energetic black
and white pups who would grow up to be energetic
and intelligent Dogs. Rose was enchanted with the
pup, and Sky approved of Rose's new friend.
Corazon was put in charge of Naming the pup, and
she thought about it long and hard. She finally
settled on Dawn. It was simple, and dawn is always
a new start. Everyone approved.

They stayed in the Village with the Traders for a
while. Corazon's healing abilities were always
welcome, and everyone was tired from weeks on
the trail. She had a long talk with Rose's parents
about helping her learn to speak with People, and
how Dawn could help. Rose's mother and father

were so happy with the change in Rose, and they
began to have some hope for her. They told
Corazon that they were tired of searching for this
Village for Different children, and wanted to settle in
the Village they were in. It was a peaceful spot, and
the harvests were always good. The People there
were happy to have them stay, and helped them
build a place to live. Corazon agreed, telling them
that if she found that village, she would make sure
they would know.

51. Owl Meets Corazon for the Second Time

Owl loved her night time journeys. Sometimes she
hunted, and sometimes she just flew for the joy of
flight. She liked the idea that she was keeping the
Boy, Coyote, and Nika safe by checking the
Trader's path every night. Even though the
memories of Duck's Village had faded back into the
past where they needed to be, Owl still wanted to
be very sure they weren't being followed. Besides,
she was getting a little bit frustrated with her male
travelling companions. They were spending their
days climbing the cliffs along the endless water,
gazing into tide pools, teaching Nika how to tell
jokes, and in general not moving forward. Owl, on
the other hand, was more than ready to move on -
she liked having a purpose. She had an idea about
which direction to take, but the others waved her
away, saying that they just weren't ready yet.

So she flew in ever-widening spirals through the night. It was cool and clear. The hunting had been good, and her belly was full. Now she was simply flying to enjoy flying. She saw a small campfire along the trail the Traders used, and was curious about who would be out in the woods all alone. While the woods were safe, most People did not see it that way, and a single campfire was a rarity. She swooped silently towards the cheerful little light in the deep night. Owls can be silent when they need to be - that's why they are such good hunters. She saw a young woman sitting on the ground. Her eyes were closed,and her hands were open on the earth. She seemed to be in deep thought, and Owl was intrigued. Most People she had seen spent little time thinking, and far too much time talking nonsense. She gave a little hoot of surprise, recognizing Corazon. She also saw what seemed to be a very small Wolf - black and white and with only three legs.

Sky, like all Dogs, had very keen hearing. She heard the soft swoosh of Owl's wings, and opened her bright blue eyes, looking directly at Owl perched lightly on a nearby branch. Owl gave a very soft hoot, meaning hello. "I know your Person." she said softly. "She helped us get away from Duck's Village. She's a very good Person, and I am happy to see her. My friends will be happy as well. Where are you going?"

Sky howled back, equally softly so as to not disturb Corazon. "My Person is on some sort of search for knowledge. She wants to travel and learn and help other People and Animals. We have had many adventures since we started, that's for sure."

Owl just kept staring at this beautiful Dog. She'd never seen a canid so lovely. Finally, she just blurted out, "I shouldn't ask, but you're missing a leg. What happened?" then she lowered her head, "That was rude. I am sorry!"

Sky snorted. She had been three-legged for so long that it wasn't even important to her any more. "No worries." she said. "When I was a very small Pup, I got caught in a Trapper's left behind Trap. It hurt a lot. My Person found me and saved my life. I am indebted to her, and I do love her."

Owl hooted back,"Thank you for telling your story. She is, indeed, a good Person. And in my limited experience, good People are rare. What is she doing? She is not asleep, but she is certainly not awake."

Sky replied proudly, "She is learning how to listen to and speak with all of life. She used to be deaf to me, but she is learning fast. It's good that at least one Person can speak with us. Right now she is listening to how the Trees speak with each other."

Owl smiled a little Owlish smile at that. "We have a Boy", she hooted. "He doesn't have a name, but he speaks with us all the time. We are traveling, too. We are a Coyote, our Boy, and a very young Wolf. Our Boy is one of what People call the Different children. But he's not so different. Maybe your Person would like to travel with us? Frankly, I have been traveling with all males for a long time now, and as much as I love them, sometimes it's all about the burp and fart jokes. I could certainly enjoy more civilized discourse, that's for sure."

Sky grinned hugely. She had seen many Boys in their travels, and yes, it could get a bit repetitious. "Let's try to talk with Corazon. She still understands like a little one, but I'll try. I think it's a wonderful idea."

Sky trotted over to Corazon, and gave her a gentle nudge with her nose. Corazon opened her eyes and stretched. She smiled. "It was so good listening to the Trees talking, Sky. They have so much knowledge and they are all interconnected. It's wonderful." Sky nudged her again, then looked in Owl's direction. Owl flew down and stood in front of Corazon. She gave a gentle little hoot - sometimes People were afraid of Owls, thinking them to be bad spirits. Owl was certainly not a bad spirit. What she was was small and fluffy. Corazon reached out her hand. "Hello, Friend Owl", she said quietly. "What brings you here? I've been hearing stories of a group of Travelers at the Rim of the World. Do you know of them?" Sky yipped happily and Owl hooted in excitement. "Yes, yes, yes!!!" she hooted in excitement, "Will you join us? We need to continue our journey, but I can't get the Boy to choose a direction. Will you come with us? Please?"

While Corazon didn't understand everything Owl was saying, she got most of it. She got a picture of the shaggy-haired skinny Boy with slanted green eyes trembling and afraid in the cave in Duck's Village. She laughed in pure joy. "That Boy is alright? I hoped he would be. He was so very sweet and brave. Sky and I would be honored to join your travelers. We'll be Clan Traveler, and we will travel far and learn much. I'm ready."

And just like that, she packed up her little camp, made sure the fire was safely out, and they were on their way to meet the Boy, Coyote, and Nika. One of the many things Corazon had learned recently was the value of the gift of the moment. She saw the moment she'd been looking for, and took it. Owl flew under the tree branches to guide them, and they moved quickly and quietly through the dark woods. All three were filled with excitement, and all three were eager to be on their way.

52. Owl Anticipates

They walked towards where the Sun went down throughout the night. Corazon was too excited to even think about sleep, but finally, just before dawn she simply had to stop. She told Owl to fly back to the travelers, and tell them of her arrival. She then pulled a blanket out of her pack and curled up to(sleep with Sky. She had not felt so full of purpose since she had decided to leave her Village.

Owl headed back to the Boy, Coyote and Nika, feeling like she was going to burst with happiness. Now, she thought, the journey could go forward.

53. The Boy Runs Away

Owl woke her friends up and breathlessly told them what had happened. Coyote, the social being that he was, was excited about new travelers to their group. Nika solemnly nodded agreement. Pack was always good.

The Boy, however, crunched up his face, stuck out his lower lip, stomped his foot and yelled, "NO! NO PEOPLE! I don't LIKE People, they have done nothing other than HURT me. I don't trust any Person, no matter how nice they seem. People threw me out to live with the Animals. And that is who I am, I am not part of Clan People. EVER!" And right in front of his shocked friends, he ran away as fast as a frightened deer.

Coyote went to follow, but Owl landed on his shoulder to stop him, "Stop now." she hooted, "Our Boy is hurting. He is remembering how hard his life was before he found us. He doesn't want to lose us to another person. He is a sensible being - let him figure it out." Coyote found not following the Boy to be very difficult, but he saw Owl's wisdom. He called out to Nika, "Pup, we need a good run to clear our heads. Let's go!" Nika didn't understand any of this, so a run seemed like the best thing to do. They went off, not to follow the Boy, but to stay out of sight and be around in case they were needed.

Owl sighed. This was not what she had expected, and she was worried about the Boy's reaction. She sent out a loving thought to her Boy, tucked her head under her wing, and went to sleep. Tonight would be interesting, to say the least.

The Boy ran and ran, hot tears sheeting down his face. He didn't want to have to deal with People. He was only a little guy, and he had been through enough. He was simply at the end of what he could adapt to, so he ran away. He pounded along the beach, kicking up white water, and howling at the top of his lungs. Had a Person seen him at this time they most certainly would have felt he was a demon.

Well, tears always run out. Legs get tired. The Boy sat down by a crystalline little tide pool and took a deep breath. He looked at his reflection in the pool. Maybe he could make a scary face and Corazon would go away. That had certainly worked before with People. So he looked at himself in the pool and tried making terrifying faces. He growled a little bit. Just to make his point. That was it, he thought, he would simply scare the interloper away. He could do that. He was getting really very impressed with his truly frightening faces when a shadow fell over the pool. The boy figured it was Coyote and Nika coming to find him, so he just continued making faces. He would impress Coyote and Nika with his fearsomeness as well.

Oddly, he heard deep and warm laughter instead of Coyote and Nika's familiar voices. So he rolled over onto his back and looked up. He was scared, but he decided to be scarier than he was scared, so he made the most horrific face he could yank his face around into making. He saw a lovely tall Woman. Not old, not young and with flowers in her hair. She looked like no person the boy had ever seen, and something in his heart flipped over.

Without a thought, a single small word in People-speak fell out of his mouth. "Mama?" he whispered. He clapped his hand firmly over his mouth and continued to stare.

The Woman shook her hair and laughed again, "Dear Boy, I only wish I had the honor of you being my son. Your life would have been very different, and that is truth. No, your Mother left you at the edge of the Forest to live or die. You looked so Different to her, and she was very young and very afraid. Just like right now you are afraid. We don't make good choices when we are scared, and she did not make a good choice." She watched as the Boy's eyes welled up and over with tears, and she continued, "Come over here and sit with me. We need to talk about who you are." She sat on a big rock and held out her arms.

The Boy was going to run away, but then he saw the two Wolves with her. Much as he loved Coyote, the gravitas of Nika had brought out in him a love and respect for Clan Wolf. He felt safe looking at the two Wolves, so he walked over to the Woman intending to stand tall and dignified like a true warrior. Instead, he threw himself into her lap, snuggling his head into her shoulder. He sighed deeply, feeling a weight he did not know he carried leave him.

The Woman sang a little song she had sung to her own children when they were frightened. The Boy snuggled even more. The older Silver Wolf came over and licked the Boy's tiny ear gently, and the Boy dug his fingers deeply into his thick coat and sighed like someone who has finally come home after a long and difficult journey.

"Dear Boy, please listen to my words. I am a friend of Coyote's, and I am the one who brought Nika to you. Your life is not a mistake. As I have said before, and as someone will say in a different Time, God does not play dice with the universe. You can ask Coyote about that. " the Boy pulled away, looking at her. His greenish eyes were luminous. No Person had ever spoken like this to him before.

"I'll continue. Corazon is a good Person, and she and Sky will complete your Clan of Travelers. You have learned from my good friend Coyote, you have learned from Owl, and you have learned from Nika. You learned from Redbird, although you don't remember that. Yet. Now, it is time for you to learn about reaching out to the People world. It needs you. You saw Duck, and he is a sickness that will spread if not stopped. You are to be part of a new way of being, and Mother Earth brought you here to teach others. Please hear me and welcome your friend Corazon - she is learning just like you are."

The Boy shrugged. He wasn't sure. But the Woman was healing a hurting spot in him he had never looked at, or even known was there. Haltingly, he said, "Can you be my mother? Just pretend? I am listening, you know."

The Woman sighed. She did not know if she was happy or sad, so she decided to be happy. "Boy, I will act as your Mother, because you have none. You are not my son, but I will always see you as my son."

The Boy gave his sunshine-on-snow bright smile and clapped his hands. The Woman gently touched his button nose and continued, "Boy, Coyote and Nika are looking for you. They are worried. Your friend Owl loves Corazon, and is saddened that you ran off. Now, you go, and you welcome Corazon.

Your purpose might not be clear to you, but it is clear to Mother Earth, and I act as her liaison. Now, go!"

The Boy gave the Woman one last hug, and quickly turned around, startling the Silver Wolf with a big kiss on his black nose. He ran back down the beach the way he had come, turning around now and then to wave at the Woman. She waved back until he was out of sight. Then she sighed, and looked at her Wolves. "I'm sorry, dear Elder Wolf. I did not know he was going to do that." The Silver Elder shook his massive head and snorted. He hadn't really minded, he growled. Just a little unexpected. The Woman smiled. "That was good work. Happy work. Let's go home.". And so they did.

54. Corazon Arrives

When Owl awoke, the Boy was standing by the tree she was resting in, looking at her intently. As soon as she opened her eyes, he blurted out, "Owl, I was wrong. I was scared and I ran away because I was afraid that Corazon would become everyone's new friend, and I would be forgotten." Then he added, "Forgotten again. I do not wish to lose the little family I have."

Owl nodded, and flew down to perch on his shoulder. She nuzzled her beak along his face, saying softly, "Boy, family never forgets family. Love is not a bucket that will become empty. It's more like this endless water we have been living by. Love is so big that it can't be emptied. You are our Family, and we will never leave you."

The Boy ruffled up Owl's feathers (revealing how really tiny she was under all that fluff.), and grinned hugely. "Well then, it's done." he laughed, "Go and get our newest member of Clan Traveler! We will see you again in the early dawn!"

Coyote and Nika had been watching and waiting and hoping for this moment. The Boy would not talk about how he had come to this insight, but they were relieved that he had. After all, he was Pack, and you never walk away from Pack. They ran circles around the boy, laughing happily the way that only canids do. "We were so worried about you!" Yipped Coyote, "Owl told us to let you figure it out on your own and for us to not follow you. I am so glad you came back!". Nika gave a low grumble, saying to the Boy, "I had no Pack, and now I am part of Clan Traveler. You are a part of us, and no one else can ever be who you are. I am glad you made the choice you did. We are family, and family is like Pack. We stay together." The Boy looked at Nika, startled. Nika rarely spoke, so when he did speak, you tended to really pay attention. The Boy sat down on the ground, sighed a big sigh, and motioned for his friends to sit by him. "I ran away because I was afraid." He said calmly. "I have never known a family until I happened along you - I was afraid of losing that. Now I know better. " He gave both his friends a gentle hug. While Coyote loved hugs and belly scratches, Nika was rather reserved about hugs, and the Boy respected that. "Thank you, friends." he sighed. "Now, let's get ready for Corazon's arrival. I am thinking some roasted rabbit might be a very good thing." Coyote and Nika heartily agreed and they all went to work creating a happy arrival for Corazon and Sky.

While they prepared for Corazon's arrival, they began to think their separate thoughts about People. Nika was too young to have had contact with them, but he had been told what had happened to his pack. He was unsure if People were to be trusted at all. He knew The Boy was a Person, but he did not really see the Boy as that, he was simply Pack. Coyote, for all of his deep pain because of People was still a trusting soul (jokesters usually are), and he was excited to meet up with a good Person. That's how Coyote was - always willing to give that next chance in the hope that this time things would be better. The Boy was torn. He had no memory of family, no memory of anything other than fear, dislike and the occasional bowl of food from People. He trusted Owl, knowing she would not bring any danger to them, but he was wondering if maybe Owl was a little too trusting. After all, she had never known People. Owls are very devoted, and they love deeply. Owl did not carry the weight of memory that the Boy, Coyote and Nika shared. The silence began to get very heavy, so the Boy decided to break it and speak.

"Coyote?" He said, "What do you think about this? At first I was excited, and yet now, I'm a little worried. Should I be?" Coyote paused to scratch behind his ear, always a good way to gather your thoughts. "Well, I don't think so, Boy." he said, "After all, Corazon did get you out of that cave and back to us. That should tell you something. Perhaps not all People are the same. We should give her a chance." Nika, having heard the tale of the Cave several times, nodded solemnly. "Any Person who would take a risk like that for you would have to be good. Right? Anyway, that's my thinking on it. Not knowing much about People. "

The Boy sighed, and went back to skinning the Rabbits Nika and Coyote had caught for them. "It seems sometimes that the past is more in the now than it should be. It's like a cloudy day, and you forget about the Sun. All you can see are clouds." Coyote looked at the Boy and blinked his golden eyes. That was, he thought, a sad and true statement.

He trotted over to the Boy and looked into his strange greenish, brownish slanted eyes. "Boy", he said quietly. "Maybe it's more like you're carrying rocks. It's hard to move forward when you're lugging around a bunch of rocks. We can't just pretend that bad things did not happen, but sometimes, we just should not continue to carry all those rocks. Let's give Corazon a chance. I am thinking this is a good thing for our Pack. Let's put down those old rocks and try something new." The Boy smiled a little, and hugged his friend. "For a Jokester, you are rather wise." he laughed. Coyote grinned. He always enjoyed being told he was wise.

They spent the rest of the evening in quiet friendship, each one thinking their own thoughts, and telling the occasional bad joke. The Boy was also practicing in his mind a surprise he had told none of his friends about. He was feeling a little scared to try something new, but Coyote was right, you can't go forward lugging around a load of rocks.

As dawn snuck up silently, they all awoke, ready to see what the day would bring. The Boy prepared a fire, and sticks to cook the rabbit. Nika and Coyote took a run just to take a run, while the Boy also picked green plants and berries. The Boy kept looking up at the sky, watching for Owl. Finally he saw her, and he called out, "Coyote, Nika! Here she comes, let's run ahead and greet her!" And off they went.

Corazon was tired, but also excited. A well-lived life was so much about change, she thought. She could have stayed in her Village, becoming entrenched in routine and getting bitter over lost chances, yet here she was walking into an adventure. Sky agreed. She was enjoying how happy Corazon had become, and she was enjoying the thought of making new friends. Up ahead they caught sight of what appeared to be a scruffy little canid, and a larger, much more graceful one. Bringing up the rear was a figure that was both scruffy and yet graceful at the same time. Corazon felt happy tears come up in her eyes. She had doubted until this moment that she would ever see the Boy again - yet there he was. Certainly taller, and even wilder hair, but still with magic crackling all about him. She laughed, saying, "Look, Sky, there they are! This is such an adventure! Let's go meet them."

So they did. Then they all stopped, feeling a little awkward, as you sometimes do when you see folks you care about that you haven't seen in a while. The Boy cleared his throat, and began his Surprise. "Greetings to you, Corazon." he began in a raspy, halting voice. "We are happy you are here. So happy that I worked hard on learning enough People-speak so I could tell you that." Then he blushed, and looked down, feeling foolish. He didn't know his voice was so raspy and his words so mushed up. He sighed.

Corazon ran right over, and hugged him hard. "Boy! You are so smart! Look at you! You are talking People! You are so brave and so smart! I'm so glad I'm here!"

Meanwhile, Owl perched tiredly on a nearby branch watching as Coyote and Nika approached Sky. They had never seen anything like her. She looked a little like Coyote, and a little like Nika, but she was neither. Her bright blue eyes were so beautiful that neither one really noticed the missing leg. They looked at each other for what seemed to be a long time, undecided. Coyote finally broke the tension. He galloped right up to Sky, did a surprisingly graceful play bow, then galloped off so fast his legs almost tangled up underneath him. Sky understood, and took off after him. While Nika watched they ran in circles - sometimes Sky chased Coyote, sometimes Coyote chased Sky. After a while, Coyote ran up to Nika, saying, "Nika, you're too serious! Sky is a new friend! Come and run with us!" Nika shook his head, snorted, and decided to drop his dignity. He took off after Coyote and the three of them zoomed through the forest until they returned panting and tired.

The travelers walked back to their small encampment with Owl tucked safely on the Boy's shoulder. They talked about everything and anything. Every once in a while, for no apparent reason, the canids would take a few laps around the group, barking and jumping. Finally when the sun began to go down, everyone stretched, yawned and went happily to sleep. The Boy was the last to nod off, and as he watched his friends sleeping safely, he smiled. Sometimes, if we are open to change, family just happens when we least expect it to.

55. Another Somewhere is Listening

Farther away, yet still along the shining endless water she paused in her dancing and whirling. The change she had been hoping for had come into being. Things were going to move quickly now, and she was eager to begin expansion of the work that had been her life's passion. She sang out her gratitude to Mother Earth for hearing her song and sighed happily. She was eager to meet these special Travelers, and tired of waiting for her vision to be fulfilled. She took a deep breath and asked for help to move sure footedly back to her Village. It was time to prepare a welcome.

56. Corazon Hears the Chatter.

After a few days of simply relaxing from the journey, Corazon brought the idea of the next step to the others. "It's beautiful here, but we have work to be doing - we can't stay." she said to the other travelers. The Boy looked at his toes, not meeting her eyes. He knew she was right - he felt the pull of the work to be done as well. He didn't want to leave this wonderful place but, he reasoned with himself, there could be even more wonderful places to see. Corazon was right, it was time to move on. Owl smiled. She had hoped that Corazon could push Coyote and the Boy into action, and she was more than ready to move on. Nika, who was growing rapidly, was excited and eager to see what adventures were ahead.

The question remained. Which direction to go? They weren't about to head back to where the Sun came up, and they could go no further towards where the Sun went down. That left North or South. They all thought and thought on this, with no-one coming up with a reason to go either direction. It was far too important to just leave to chance. Owl flew up and down the coast at night in both directions, and could find no compelling reason to go either way. They were all troubled by this, and debated sporadically with no resolution.

One morning, Corazon decided to take a long walk by herself. She left Sky with Coyote and Nika, and the three of them went for a run. She waved to them and set off towards the water. She had gotten very comfortable with listening to the chatter of the trees, and she was going to use that to help to gain some knowledge about which direction to move in.

When she found a quiet spot she sat down, closed her eyes, and let her mind reach out. Initially, this had been so very hard for her to do, but with daily practice it was becoming easier and easier. She began to pick up on the waves of information the trees passed through their communal chatter. Some it was typical - a good rain, a new Village, or a band of travellers. Then she began to feel something different. Drumming, singing, and feet pounding into the sand. It was strong and welcoming, so she listened more deeply. She began to see a large woman with very dark skin wearing colorful clothing whirling, leaping, and falling back to earth with the lightness of a leaf. She could feel the drumming, and she heard a high, clear tenor singing about the dance, the waves, and the beauty of the day. Corazon was fascinated - she began to understand that while the two on the beach were aware of her, they posed no threat. In fact, they were wishing to meet her and Clan Traveller. She felt a welcome there, as well as much-desired knowledge.

Corazon took a deep breath, stood up, and still with eyes closed began turning slowly in the sand. She would know the direction to be taking when she stopped. After several seconds, the sound faded away, but Corazon felt a definite pull. She opened her eyes. She was facing due North. That was it. Now they had a direction, and knew they would receive a welcome. She leapt up into the air and laughed - it felt so good to finally end the constant debate and procrastination. She could hardly wait to tell the others, deciding to wait until early evening when Owl woke up. She hugged herself, thinking of the tired and earthbound person she had been just a short while ago. Her life had become an adventure, she had a Clan that she loved - and she had work she loved. She was eager to head North

and become the healer she knew she was meant to
be.

She began to walk back to the encampment when
she caught a flash of color on the edge of her
vision. Turning, she saw a bright red cardinal
perched on a nearby rock. The little bird cocked its
head and chirped. Corazon smiled back, and
silently thanked Redbird for her guidance.

57. Nika Goes Dark

As Corazon was walking back and the Boy was
watching a tide pool's endless cycle, the canids
were having a good run. Despite her missing leg,
Sky was able to run with Coyote and Nika quite
well. Many times they would sprint ahead and then
loop back to her. Sky didn't mind, it was good to be
in the company of other canids. Besides, she
enjoyed Coyote's bad jokes and Nika's precocious
solemnity.

The day was one of those golden days in early Fall,
when it seems as if there is no passing of time.
There was a light breeze, and the Sun starting to
go down was bright and warm. Everything felt clear
and bright. The three spoke little, with the ease of
old friends who don't need to talk all the time. They
came to a meadow filled with wildflowers and sweet

grass. As one, the three decided to do what canids do and enjoy a good roll in grass. Laughing, they rolled around, got up, shook, and began to go forward.

A doe and her fawn trotted into the meadow, both also enjoying the day. Coyote and Sky looked at them with interest, but no desire to chase. Nika began to feel something he had not felt before, something strong and dark and blind. He had hunted rabbits with Coyote for food, but that had simply been about eating, and he wasn't even hungry right now. This was different, very different. He just wanted to kill because he wanted to kill. He didn't understand this urge, but he was powerless to stop it. He went belly to the long grass, ears back and utterly silent. He moved purposefully toward the doe and fawn who were unaware of his presence. It wasn't winter, the herd was not starving and there should be nothing to fear from Clan Wolf.

Part of Nika's mind was screaming. Killing just to kill was a sin for any member of the canid Clans. There was a strict pact with Clan Deer that they would only give up their lives for food in the dead of Winter to feed the Wolves, and to cull the herd so the Deer could survive. Nika buried that thought as the air around him seemed to get darker and darker becoming the color of blood long spilled. The air was heavy and Nika moved through it like a hawk cutting through the space. Seamlessly flowing, he moved closer to the doe and her fawn. His teeth moved back from his lips, his pupils became large, eyes glowing. He was both terrifying and beautiful in that moment. Coyote and Sky were horrified, yet could not look away. Coyote tried to call out, but the call dried up and died in his throat.

 Nika leapt. Horror and grace in one fluid movement. The doe met eyes with him, first startled, then truly afraid. She nudged her fawn behind her and did the only thing she could, bringing her sharp hooves down onto Nika's head. Not expecting this, Nika moved back a step, shook himself and began to move forward again. The doe pushed her fawn ahead of her and began to do what deer do - she ran. Nika pursued. The fawn, being little and unsteady on its new legs began to fall behind.

Coyote was so angry with himself for standing there paralyzed. That was HIS Nika, his baby, his foster son, and Nika was about to do something so heinous he would have to be exiled from the pack. Or worse. The fawn was bleating, and the doe turned making ready for another stand. Coyote shook himself hard, trying to force himself out of this stuck moment. Say what you will about Clan Coyote, jokesters also love deeply and fiercely, doing whatever they can to preserve the pack. Coyote had always felt that he had betrayed his pack by not being there when the Trappers came. Now he had another chance, and he was not about to let it go by while he watched passively. He jumped up in the air, shaking himself wildly, and he fell to earth running like the North wind tearing up a winter landscape.

Coyotes aren't really very big. They think they are, and they are large in their stories, but Coyote was smaller than Sky, and certainly much smaller than Nika. That was not going to deter Coyote. As he ran he was thinking as quickly as only a jokester can think. What could he do? Nika was large now, and very strong. He could see that something dark and just plain wrong had gotten hold of Nika and he did not feel that he was looking at his foster pup anymore. He finally gave up on trying to think his way out of this one and said, "Spirit, here I go. Guide me. Please. I have to do the right thing here." He pulled up all of his energy, jumped as high as he could, and crashed down right on top of Nika.

Nika was startled. To put it mildly. His thoughts had been all dark and bloody with the sound of ripping flesh and breaking bones. Then this furry weight fell on top of him. He whipped around staring at Coyote, not recognizing his foster father at all. Coyote was terrified. Where was his gentle and precocious baby Nika? What was this monstrous thing that looked like Nika, smelled like Nika - but wasn't his Nika. Coyote just could not stand it any longer. He couldn't lose another pack, he just could not. He began to bark fiercely at Nika, trying to talk some sense into him. Nika just stared at him for a while, then turned back towards the doe and fawn who were almost to the safety of the woods. He snorted. He could catch them easily. He gathered himself up, preparing to run.

At that moment the whole world seemed to crash down on top of him. The air whoosed out of him in a painful gasp. Not like little Coyote who had simply bounced off of Nika's strong back. This was a being of at least equal weight, smarter and more powerful than him. He felt teeth on the back of his neck and heard a strong growled message from the weight on top of him.

"End this now, little Nika. Your life is in my jaws. If you do not stop this madness now, you are no longer Pack. I will dispose of you happily. There is no place for murdering rouges here. Stop now." The voice descended into a growl so low and deep that Nika felt the earth under his body vibrate.

While this was happening, Coyote was shaking and feeling relieved at the same time. Tears were unashamedly running down his face. What Nika wasn't able to see was that the presence pinning him down was the Woman's Silver Wolf. The Golden Wolf stood nearby ready to move in if

needed. They were quietly and totally in control of
Nika. Coyote's ever-rational mind was screaming at
the improbability of two large and rather
preternatural Wolves just showing up out of thin air
at exactly the right time but he rationalized that he
had certainly seen stranger things on this journey.
Honestly, he was just overjoyed that they had
shown up at all. He'd take the intervention with no
questions asked. He sighed and looked around.
Maybe the Woman had arrived as well. He could
certainly stand jumping into her arms for a
puppy-hug right now. He was shaking and crying,
and just could not stop. He was praying to whatever
gods Coyotes pray to that Nika would be alright
again, because he could not stand the thought of
losing his foster son. He scanned around, ears
tilting wildly listening and searching for her.

He finally saw her at the edge of the forest,
whispering to the doe and her fawn. She gave the
doe a loving little smack on her rump and off they
leapt into the welcome safety of the woods. She
turned, saw Coyote and opened her arms,
beckoning him to come. Coyote didn't need a
second invite. Even though he was still shaking and
crying he ran as fast as a summer thunderstorm
and jumped up like a Pup into her arms.

After a bit of puppy-snuggling and snuffling up his
tears, Coyote turned to look at his beloved friend.
"The question begs itself," he snuffled, "What just

happened here?" He carefully glanced over to where the Silver Wolf had Nika still pinned unmoving on the ground. What's going on? That being said, I am surely happy you showed up, that's truth."

The Woman ruffled the scruffy fur on Coyote's head and gently put him back on the ground. "Well, the future is never set in stone.", she sighed wearily. "I don't know what happened to Nika. It does happen once in a while during times of great famine. Good Wolves just break from the constant hunting and the hunger and become rogue killers. The Pack has to dispose of them - even exile can't help them." Coyote shuddered, thinking of the powerful jaws still bearing down on Nika's neck. "What about my baby Nika?", he cried. "I can't lose him. He's so wonderful and special and quietly funny and he loves me and he carries stuff for the Boy even though he thinks it's stupid to need stuff and he has a big crush on Sky and he thinks Owl is beautiful and he thinks Corazon is magical and he's MY BABY." he wailed. He began snuffling again, hating himself for being so emotional in front of his friend, but unable to stop.

"I know." said The Woman, "I know. There is some sort of evil running loose on Mother Earth. I had thought it defeated when Duck was defeated, but like a stink bug, it just showed up somewhere else. We will do everything we can do to heal our Nika, don't fear." She gave Coyote a hug and smiled a very tired smile. "The future is mutable, and God does not play dice with the Universe." Coyote gave back an equally tired smile. "You keep saying that." he sighed.

The two walked slowly over to where Nika lay, still pinned and immobile on the ground. Although he looked at him every day, Coyote was shocked to see how much Nika had grown. He remembered the eager and funny little pup with the huge ears sleeping on his back as he trotted back to the Boy. He remembered how he and the Boy had taught Nika about making jokes, and how Nika's jokes were always smart-jokes. Jokes you had to think about before you laughed. Coyote liked that about Nika. He liked how Nika was always the last one to go to sleep - waiting to make sure the others were all safe. He liked how Nika would save the best parts of a rabbit for Owl when she came home in the dawn, always waking up to greet her. He liked the way Nika, big as he was, could pad silently through the woods, and hear everything going on around him. He looked at The Woman with a big unspoken question in his eyes. Could Nika ever be Nika again? The Woman looked back and her look said she did not know. Coyote stared at his toes, then looked up at The Woman. "You gave me Nika to care for as my own." he said, "And I am going to do my best to see him healed from this." The Woman nodded in agreement. She called out to the

Silver Wolf to let Nika up. When the Silver Wolf resisted, her voice became firm. "He cannot stay under your jaws forever, we need to see if our Nika is back, or if he is still a monster. If he is still a monster, I know you can dispatch him easily." The Silver Wolf slowly backed away, grumbling. Coyote found he was holding his breath. He wanted to know - and yet he did not want to know.

Nika stood up on unsteady legs. The adrenaline that had fueled his madness was gone now, and he was feeling shaky and sick. Coyote walked fearlessly up to him, stood right in front of his massive jaws and said, "My son, are you still our NIka? Or are you something else - I have to know even if you kill me where I stand. Are you still our Nika?"

There was a long pause while Nika drew several gasping breaths. He hurt all over, and he had little memory of what had happened to him, save that it was very bad. He had almost killed the fawn when there was no need for food. He shuddered, and looking at his foster father whispered, "I don't know what happened to me. I knew it was wrong. I went away somewhere. I was far away from who I am. I don't deserve to be a part of this clan anymore." He turned to the Silver Wolf and bared his throat. "I deserve to die - I betrayed the pact with Clan Deer. " The silver Wolf looked at The Woman, waiting for direction. She shook her head. "Come here, not-so-little Nika, we will talk about this. I am thinking you were caught up by something larger, something that wants your sweet spirit and bright mind out of the world. The same something that captured the Boy and controls Snake." She sat down and motioned for Nika to sit by her.

Coyote sat by her side, and the two Wolves lay down patiently to watch. Nika felt as if the whole of Mother Earth was watching him - and judging. He was about to make excuses, rationalize what had happened, and then decided not to. He had done what he had done - had Coyote and the Silver Wolf not intervened he would have been covered in blood he could never wash off. So he simply sat and looked The Woman straight in the eye. "I know what I did." he said softly. "I know that in many ways, it wasn't really me, but that just sounds like an excuse. I should have been stronger." Coyote was holding back from running to Nika and giving him a comforting ear wash. This was Nika's time to grow up. It was not what Coyote had wanted for him, but here it was. This was Nika's to deal with.

The Woman held Nika's large head in her callused and capable hands. Hands that had seen birth, death, harvest and famine. Nika just let his big head drop,the grief of what he had almost done overwhelming him. "Nika, Little Brother, I am seeing now that there was a larger power at work here." murmured The Woman into his ear. "In your true heart and mind, you would never have thought of doing such a thing. Coyote was brave to try and stop you. He is a true father to you, and I am glad you are growing up with him to guide you. I came to intervene. To try and save you from destroying yourself by your actions, whatever force motivated them. We did that, and now it is time to move on. We now know that this power did not pass with Duck. It is still here, and we will be on guard."

Nika was still a Pup in many ways, even though he was so large and strong. He snuggled into The Woman, and whimpered a little. "Is it at all possible that I can still be Pack?" he whispered, not wanting Coyote to hear, "I will always be aware now, and I will not let that happen ever again. Really. I promise. I don't want to lose my friends. Can Coyote forgive me?" well, Coyote did not have huge dish-like ears for nothing, he heard every word, and just could not contain himself sitting sedately any longer. He bounced over to NIka and gave him a head-butt. Nika turned startled, and all Coyote saw in his eyes was Nika's loving and gentle soul. Coyote licked Nika's face. "Of course you are forgiven" he yipped. "You certainly gave us a scare, that's for sure. But we had help!" he said as he grinned at The Woman and nodded respectfully to her Wolves, "And it seems that we have work to be doing. This evil has no place on Mother Earth, and we must do something, anything to heal it." he yipped a laugh, thinking himself very witty, "It's a Quest! It used to be a Journey, and now it's a Quest!" Nika had to laugh a little at this. Coyote always had such a way of making things sound grand and exciting. For his part, he really did not want to be face to face with that evil ever again. However, he decided that keeping quiet right now was the best thing to do. After all, he had his Pack back, and that was all he wanted. He was so tired, and he decided that for a little while, it would be alright to be a Pup again. He lowered his head into The Woman's lap, sighing, "If you don't mind, I'd really like to take a nap now, thank you so much for showing up, and thank your Wolves, too. Although my neck still hurts a bit." With that, he fell deeply and peacefully asleep.

58. Sky Sings and the Clan Assembles

Everyone had forgotten about Sky. She stood in the meadow, watching the scene unfold. She didn't know if she should try to help Nika or run away and hide. Like Coyote, she was paralyzed by seeing something so horrific that she just could not comprehend it. Nika would never try to kill a fawn, that was just not who he was. He could have killed Coyote as well. She felt as if the sun had been put out like a small campfire and she was standing all alone in a very dark world. When she saw the two Wolves arrive, she was sure her friend Nika would be no more. Certainly they were sent to stop him, and she began to grieve for her friend. Finally, when she saw Nika fall peacefully asleep in The Woman's lap she let out a breath she did not know she'd been holding. Coyote and Nika were acting like they knew this Person, so she must be a good Person. The Wolves were intimidating - but then, most Wolves are. Sky began to move towards the group, not sure if she would be welcome or not. Coyote saw her, and barked out, "Sky, come over here! I want you to meet our friend!" he looked warily at the Wolves, "Uh, and her friends, too! Come, Sky."

Sky looked at the group. And like our emotions often do, the enormity of what had just happened hit Sky unexpectedly. Like Coyote had done, she began to tremble, and she felt tears begin their way down her face, falling on the ground. They had almost lost their Nika, their Little Brother. Like the rest of her group, Sky was an orphan. For a long time, Corazon had been her whole world, and now her world had opened up to include the Boy, Owl, Nika and Coyote. She could not imagine losing any of them. The emotions rushed through her like a windstorm, as she stood there looking at her two dear friends and The Woman. Like Coyote and Nika, she felt an overwhelming urge to turn her face up to the sky and howl when things were just bigger than she could understand. So she did. Unlike Coyote's and Nika's howls, Sky's was more like a Song winding up and up into the bright blue sky that matched her eyes. It slid down into a grumble, and up into a high trembling warble. She sang and sang about her love for her friends, her horror at what had happened to Nika, her fear that she would lose both Nika and Coyote, and then her relief that both were going to be alright. She sang her gratitude to The Woman and her Wolves for somehow showing up at exactly the right moment. She sang about their journey, and the excitement she woke up with every day. She sang for a long time, while the group just listened.

From farther away, Corazon heard Sky's song as well. She couldn't understand all of it, but she knew that something bad had happened to Nika, and she was afraid. She began to run towards the meadow, fearing what she would see there.

The Boy heard Sky's song, and he understood it better than Corazon. Nika - what had happened to Nika? He jumped up and also began to run.

In her daytime sleep, Owl heard Sky. At first she thought it was a dream - Nika doing something as horrendous as to try and kill just to kill? It had to be a dream. She slowly opened her eyes, squinting a little at the bright daylight. No, it wasn't a dream. Something had really happened. She fluffed her feathers, trying to wake up fully. Then she began to fly swiftly to the meadow.

The three found each other. They looked at each other, afraid to go forward, but needing to know what had occurred. The Boy grabbed Corazon's hand for comfort, and she squeezed his hand back - she was afraid, too. They saw Owl and began to follow her.

When they arrived at the meadow, Corazon did not even waste time to stop and look around. She saw Sky and ran to her, hugging her hard. The Boy saw Nika sleeping peacefully with his head in The Woman's lap, and he saw Coyote ginning his huge grin at the sight of the Boy. Coyote ran up to the Boy and said, "Nika wasn't our Nika - something terrifying happened to him. It was like the scary People in Duck's Village talking about how you were a Demon and how they were going to kill you.

It was like that. I was scared, really, really scared, but I tried to stop Nika. I just bounced off of him, though. Then the Wolves showed up, poof, out of nowhere. I don't know how they did that, but they were able to stop Nika. And my friend The Woman showed up, poof, out of nowhere, too. See? There she is. She's magic, I know. Come and meet her."

Well, the Boy needed no introduction to The Woman - she had filled that empty spot where we all need our Mother, and he was the better for it. He smiled, hugged Coyote and said, "You can tell your story tonight when we sit around the fire. I am sure your part in this story will grow much bigger in your mind until then. Let's go check on Nika!" With that, he ran up to The Woman, his strange face becoming beautiful in his joy.

The Woman returned his smile, her tired face becoming beautiful as well. Happiness does that to us - when we are happy and with the beings we love, we become beautiful. There is no paint or potion that can make us as lovely as joy does. "Hello, Boy" said The Woman. "I wasn't anticipating seeing you again so soon, but here we are. Nika was saved, and he is our Little Brother again. But we have a bigger thing to discuss. Coyote is correct. We had all thought that the evil running around on Mother earth was defeated when Duck was defeated - now we have found that is not so. We need to talk about your journey, and it is time for you to move on. Corazon has the direction you seek. Come and sit by me. We will wait here for Corazon and sleepy Owl, and then we will discuss this." The Boy nodded, and plopped down next to her. He rested his head on her shoulder and began gently stroking Nika's huge head. Nika smiled a little in his sleep, knowing he was safe and his friends were all around him. Owl whooshed in sleepily, saw all was well, landed on the Boy's shoulder putting her head under her wing and promptly went back to sleep again. She knew she'd hear all about it later.

Healer that she was, Corazon checked Sky all over. Sky kept telling her that she was really just fine, and tried to explain what had happened. All Corazon understood was that it was a lot like what had happened in Duck's Village, and a lot like Snake with her lies. That made her feel cold and scared. She looked around as if expecting Duck to waddle in on his tiny feet at any second, or Snake to move silently out of the woods, bulging eyes glaring. Then she saw The Woman. Healers always recognize other Healers, and Corazon knew The Woman was a true shaman as well as a Healer. From where she stood with Sky in the meadow, she gave a low and ceremonial bow, acknowledging who The Woman was. The Woman called out to her, "Corazon, you are a great healer as well. Don't bow to me, we are equals. Come here, we will use this time together to discuss your journey and what it now means. I sense you have found the right direction to take. We want to hear! Come and join us." Corazon cast a wary look at the two Wolves, but Coyote pitched in, "Don't be afraid, Corazon, I won't let them hurt you! I know these guys!", and quickly became silent as both Wolves turned to regard him cooly.

So they sat and talked. They all saw now that there was certainly a force to be reckoned with loose in the world, and they were in agreement that there had to be a way to heal Mother Earth from its influence. While it was a serious discussion, it was also a loving one. Each being felt, maybe for the first time, that they were unique and an important part of this healing. The Boy's usually fierce face relaxed into his sweet smile as he began to understand who he was. Corazon's tense shoulders dropped and she saw that she could release her burden of having to make everything just fine for everyone. Sky saw that despite her missing leg (or perhaps because of it), she was truly whole, and that her devotion to Corazon and her friends was her strength. Coyote saw that jokes are power and can carry their own kind of healing to others. Owl, in her sleep, dreamt that she wasn't a tiny barn Owl, she was a giant and beautiful force riding the night sky, protecting her friends. In his sleeping, Nika felt the power of Clan Wolf - a power that unites the seen and the unseen worlds. He sighed contentedly, feeling whole in his spirit again.

He knew now for certain that the darkness would never take him over. Each being saw clearly who they were, and how they fit into a Plan that was so large that while they knew they were a part of it, they could not see the Plan in its entirety.

The Sun began its path down into the great water, and The Woman motioned that it was time to rise and get on with their work. She gave each traveller a warm hug, whispering a blessing that was just for them into their ears. She told them to go back to their camp, have supper, and talk about continuing their journey. The group began to walk back to their camp, each one feeling strong and complete in who they were. They talked very little, turning their thoughts over in their minds. When Coyote turned back at the edge of the forest to see The Woman just one more time, she was gone. He chuckled quietly, wondering just how she and the Wolves accomplished that wonderful trick, but not really caring. Somehow, it was just fine that he did not know.

59. A Father-Son Conversation

When they got back to their camp, Corazon made her announcement - they were going to head North, and she wanted to get going right away. She was excited by what she had seen, and the others became excited with her. They built a fire, and sat around the bright flames talking happily about their next step.

Except for the Boy. He sat quietly, thinking about watching his tide pools, climbing trees, and jumping into the endless water to cool off on a hot day. He wasn't sure at all that he wanted to leave this place. He knew that he had a Bigger Purpose, but why, he thought, couldn't he just fulfill it here? Just like he'd been doubtful about Corazon's arrival, he was doubtful about moving on. But, as a small voice only he could hear explained, Corazon was now a friend and he valued her company - he brushed that thought aside, refusing to look at it. He just did not want a change.

Most of the time, the Boy was a very happy Person. After all, he was no longer alone, he had friends he could explore with, tell bad jokes with, and snuggle up to at night while watching the stars. For the first time in his life, he felt safe and loved. Change is always scary - but it has to happen, that's just the way the Mother made her world. The harvest in the Fall gave you food through the Winter. The long

slumber of the Winter prepared the world for the abundance of Spring. The long days of the Summer gave you time to prepare for the harvest in the Fall. Without change, there would be no growth. The Boy knew this, but he also did not want to leave a place where he felt happy and safe. So he looked at his toes while the others were eagerly chattering away, and he grumbled a little bit. A very quiet gumble, but we all know that Coyote did not have those big years for nothing. He heard the grumble and glanced over at the Boy. He saw a face that he did not see often, but one he knew well when he saw it. He called it the Mule Face - because it meant that the Boy was going to plant his feet onto the ground, look down at his toes, and refuse to move or even listen. Just like a Mule.
Coyote was the Boy's first and best friend. He would happily do anything to make sure the Boy was safe and to know that he was loved beyond measure. He had always seen the Boy as a large and hairless Pup, considering himself the Boy's father as well as Nika's. He never told the Boy this, but maybe it was time for him to have a father-like talk with the Boy. That Mule Face was not going to do the travellers any good, and nobody would consider leaving the Boy behind.

So he got up, stretched, yawned and said, "Hey, I need to move around a little before I go to sleep. Want to come on a walk with me?"

The Boy did not look up. "No." was all he said.
Coyote knew this response well. If he persisted, it
would be an endless string of "no" getting
progressively louder and more defiant. He decided
to work around it and get the Boy to walk with him.
"I was just wondering if you had ever looked at the
tide pools in the starlight. I think I'm going to go
there now and see what they're like at night. I have
a feeling they'll be magical. Want to come along?"

The Boy looked up, shaking his heavy, shaggy hair.
"Maybe", he said, slitting up his eyes (only adding
to the Mule face - Coyote was trying hard not to
laugh.) "I'll think about it."

Coyote began to move out of the light of the
campfire. "Well, I'll see you later, then." And he
began to trot off.

"Wait, wait! I want to see the tide pools, too! Wait!
I'm coming." The Boy stood up and followed
Coyote.

Coyote smiled. The Boy did not know it, but Coyote
considered that one his very best Trick.

The two walked in a companionable silence
towards the beach. After a bit, Coyote turned and
faced the Boy, looking deep into his eyes. The Boy
glared back, saying "I know what you're going to

say. But I don't want to go somewhere new. I like it here. I don't want to go."

"You know what? Hairless Pup, I agree. It would be much easier to just stay here. It's a wonderful place, and I love it here as well. So do Corazon,Sky, and Nika. None of us really wants to leave here, and I have a feeling this will be a place we always return to - we might make it our home after we fulfill our work for Mother Earth." The Boy looked at Coyote. He had not been called "Hairless Pup" in quite a while. He was reminded that he was still a boy, and right now he needed someone to listen to how a young boy might be feeling. He looked back at Coyote, "You are my best and oldest friend, Coyote. You always make sure I'm alright, and you always try to make me laugh even when I don't want to laugh. I don't want to talk right now. I want to think about what I want to say, and then we'll talk. Let's go sit by a tide pool. I want to see if it's as magical as you say." he sighed a rather heavy sigh, "Then we'll talk. I promise."

Together, they trotted through the moonlight, found a small tide pool and sat down together. Coyote had been right. In the starlight and moonlight, the pool was truly magical to see. Both of them looked at it for a long time. Coyote felt quiet for a change, and the Boy felt pretty confused. Finally, he turned and faced his old friend. "I am afraid," he said simply. "I feel safe here. I know every tree, rock and pool. I know The Woman said I had a greater purpose, but, honestly, I think I'm scared of my purpose. What if I'm just not strong enough?"

Coyote nodded. These were emotions he understood well. He uncharacteristically decided to just be quiet and let the Boy talk. He listened, nodded, and said "I understand." until the Boy finally finished looking at all of his doubts about himself. He saw the Boy finally stand up, saying, "Coyote, you and the Woman are right. Yes, I'm scared. What if we run into another Duck? And I can't just stay here and play for always. Let's make a pact to come back here when we can. I will hold that in my heart, and I will go with you in the morning. Let's go back to the camp now." The Boy cast one more longing look at the tide pool sparkling in the night. He sighed, shook his wild hair, pushed it off of his face and looking at Coyote with clear eyes said, "Let's go, it seems that we are now part of something much bigger than our own small story. Time to move on and see who or what is waiting for us."

60. The Journey Moves North

They set out the next morning as soon as Owl had returned from her flight. She had flown North up the coastline, and was happy to report to the travellers that she saw nothing amiss or threatening. She then perched on the Boy's shoulder to sleep, and the group set off.

They moved along the shoreline. Coyote was in the lead, eyes and ears scanning the way ahead. Sky was in the center, doing the same while walking next to Corazon. Nika was in the rear, his large ears also scanning for any sound. Although he was sad to be leaving the first place he had ever felt was truly home to him, the Boy, like all Boys everywhere was excited to be on an adventure. He sort of hopped and skipped, sometimes next to Coyote (who was doing his best to remain serious but failing - like the Boy, he was caught up in a sense of adventure and excitement.), sometimes next to Nika in the back. Nika would respond with a shoulder bump and a low growl to please be a little more serious. He was trying mightily to not act like a Pup, but the Boy's enthusiasm was contagious and he was soon shoulder-bumping playfully and grinning while he brought up the rear. Corazon had her own thoughts which were about her skills as a healer, her new ability to hear all of life going on around her, and what her role would be when they reached their destination. She felt the pull North like the magnet in a compass, and she didn't know if she felt a joyful sense of anticipation, or the weight of what she would be doing. She decided to just let the thoughts rest and allow the outcome to be whatever it would be.

So the group moved along for several days. The coastline became rockier, and they often left the shoreline for the easier traveling the woods offered. They camped at night, while Owl flew further North to make sure all was well.

Corazon dreamt about the dark woman dancing on the beach every night. Sometimes they spoke, although Corazon could never remember what the conversation was when she awoke. Sometimes Corazon danced with her, sometimes she stood back and watched. While she was beginning to feel as if she knew this woman - who was a great healer, she felt that there was an aspect to her that she was missing. She wondered in her waking hours what that was, and told herself to simply wait and see. Trying to analyze this experience, difficult as that was for her, was not going to work.

The Boy, on the other hand, was all about experiencing. He knew they were going to be a part of a much bigger work, but he didn't think about that much. He was with his friends, his Clan Traveler, and after all his years of a feral existence that was more than enough. Sometimes he, Nika, and Coyote would talk about what this Work could be, and they all had different ideas. They talked, Corazon dreamed, Sky watched over Corazon, and they moved closer to their True North day by day.

61. Waiting on the Beach

Further North, the dark woman was listening intently. She stood still, facing South where the travelers would be coming from. She had summoned them, and she had been waiting for the right travelers to arrive for a long time. Now her vision would finally become reality. She turned to walk back inland, and stumbled on a rock. She stood still again, trying to not let her frustration overwhelm her. "Wren!" She called out, "Wren, where are you?"

From a small distance away, a melodious voice called back. "Khadja, I'm right here. I'm sorry I didn't see you begin to move - I was writing a song. But the song is about you, so that's alright. Right?" Khadja sighed. Wren was her helper as well as a shaman-in-training, and he was a good man. But sometimes...she stopped the thought in its frustrated tracks, shaking her head. She needed Wren, and his light outlook on life and gentle nature made him a pleasure to work with. She was angry with herself, knowing that it would do no good to be angry with herself. She held out her hand, saying, "Wren, we need to go back and prepare for the arrival of our travelers. Would you sing so I can find you?"

In agreement, Wren's clear tenor rose up into the space around them. In apology, he came over and took Khadja's hand. She nodded a wordless acceptance, and the two proceeded inland.

Wren was the first to break the silence. "It's not your fault that you lost your sight, you know. It doesn't help that you become so angry with yourself. You tried to save our village from the fever, you saved me when I was orphaned - and you lost your sight getting the sickness from trying to save us, not because of anything that was your misdoing." Khadja scowled, motioning for him to stop speaking. This was an old subject, but always a fresh wound. How could a healer and a shaman also be blind? Her limitations never failed to frustrate her, sometimes making her difficult to be around. However, Wren's loyalty and good humor never wavered.

In truth, Wren never wavered. He had grown from a sick and scrawny infant of dubious longevity into a tall and striking young man. His voice had grown with him, from a tremorous little alto into a powerful and clear tenor. Khadja often thought that while Wren might never be a visionary shaman, he was most certainly a visionary singer. When he sang, the words took on life and unfolded their stories in your imagination, opening up worlds. He had offered as a young one to be her eyes when she lost her sight due to a high fever that had ravaged their village. Khadja had worked without food or rest for weeks on end, trying to save those she could, and making immense fires to burn the bodies of those who died so the bodies would not infect those who still lived. Wren's parents among them. They had died before giving him a name. Upon hearing his voice Khadja named him. Wrens are wonderful singers, but they are also industrious and devoted. That was most certainly Wren. He rarely became angry, and if he did he simply walked away until he was himself again. His jokes were simple and easy to understand - he was no trickster. Mostly, he took care of Khadja, and he sang. He wrote songs as well, but they were so connected with the Earth that you could easily forget that someone had written them. They were just that comfortable to listen to.

The two continued back to the campsite silently wrapped up in their own thoughts. When they settled down, Wren asked, "When will they arrive? Do you know how many they are? What should we do?". Khadja thought about that. She only knew them by larger names than they would ever call themselves: Holy Child, Trickster, Wise Woman, Healer, Wounded One, and Leader. She had no idea which ones would be People, and which ones would hail from the animal kingdom. She only knew how they felt and seemed to her mind's eye. She shrugged, "Wren, I really do not know. I sense who they are, and I know that they are much more than they think they are. I would say we roast some meat, gather some greens and berries, and create a spot where they can rest. They are the Change we have been hoping for, but they don't know that."

62. The Mound

The travelers moved along the coastline for several days, camping on the beach at night. The Boy was adept at catching fish, and after a while figured out how to make a net out of woven strands of seaweed that washed up on the beach. Corazon knew how to heat stones and to cook the fish wrapped in more of the ever-present kelp. While the canids preferred their fish raw, and Owl met her own needs through her nightly hunting, the Boy and Corazon enjoyed the cooked fresh fish immensely. Often, while watching the glowing embers of the nightly fire with Nika and Coyote curled up against him, the Boy thought that whatever task awaited them could wait a long time - this traveling with his friends was most satisfying.

Most of the time when like the Boy, we sit back and congratulate ourselves on how very smoothly our life is going, life walks in with other plans. After a few days of travel, the beach became narrow, and the cliffs very steep. The travelers decided that they would need to move inland in order to escape the tides which now moved all the way up to the foot of the cliffs. They slowly worked their way up to the top of the cliffs lining the beach, finding an ancient and windswept forest. They looked in amazement at trees whose circumference was larger than any living thing they had seen before. Corazon told them that the song the trees were singing was so old, she could not comprehend it - it seemed to be the stuff the Earth was created from. They moved quietly through this place, as if afraid to disturb the ancient beings there.

At night they built a fire. Not so much for heat and light, but for a way to drive back the darkness that was so much deeper than any night they had known before. Coyote in particular thought about this special kind of darkness quite a bit. Mostly because he liked turning over puzzles in his mind, but also because he did not know if this darkness was benign, malevolent, or simply neutral towards their presence. He finally decided on neutral, but found that thought to be very disconcerting, something he chose to not share with the others. It seemed that the ancient trees watched them, but it also seemed that they did not care. They had other thoughts and other concerns.

So they slowly picked their way through the heavy undergrowth, longing for the days of easy travel along the shore. Sometimes it seemed as if the land itself wanted to prevent them from going forward, and they spent their evenings pulling out the brambles wound tightly into hair and fur. It began to get warmer, which only brought out the insects. Insects that seemed to be as large and ancient as the great trees. Nika and Coyote snapped ferociously at the flying, stinging bugs, but for every one they snapped in two, it seemed ten more appeared to take its place. Nobody was happy, and the adventure had ceased to become an adventure. They woke each morning hoping to find a way back to the ease of traveling the coastline, and went to sleep each night feeling trapped in an ancient and unforgiving place.

Nika and Coyote were pretty much fed up with the painful and slow travel. One day, they just decided to forget about the heat, brambles and bugs to have a race. Nika was big and long-legged, but Coyote was very agile so they decided that they were evenly matched. Without telling the others, off they went with a confused cloud of hungry insects trailing behind them.

Their running was hard going in the thick underbrush, and both of them fell, all tangled up more than once. But it felt so good to just feel free of the oppressive weight of the ancient trees and their quiet spell that they just didn't care. After a while, they both fell to the ground panting, laughing, and loudly debating who truly had won the race. Coyote said that he fell the fewest times, so he must be the winner. Nika said that he was the more powerful, pushing through the brush so of course he deserved the honor. They lay there in the muggy forest debating this until the others caught up.

Corazon wanted to chastise the two for taking off like that with no warning, but the Boy put a quiet hand on her arm. "Shhh. Corazon. They meant no harm. This place is so old and so full of some kind of magic we don't understand, we can't blame them. They just wanted to laugh a little." he looked at Corazon looking like the Boy he was and always would be, "I could be wanting to laugh a little bit right now, too, Corazon." Unknown to him a tear met with the sweat on his face and trickled off his button nose falling silently on to the ground. Corazon saw the tear and gave the Boy a hug. "I understand." she whispered, "We all need this part of our journey to end. Maybe soon, eh?" The Boy silently nodded, then loped off to join Nika and Coyote's debate.

Some things are begging you to find them, like a scarlet leaf settling on your foot in the Fall. Or a butterfly full of life flying by your face, just asking for your admiration. A cold winter sunset that turns the ice into fire, taking your breath away. Those things give us joy in their shout for attention. Yet the deep forest often holds things secret and hidden that are waiting to be found, too. As the three were loudly debating the winner of the race, Sky was hearing a humming so low that only her dog's keen sense of hearing registered it at all. Corazon didn't hear it, but felt the energy. She turned and looked at Sky with a question. Sky barked once, moving away and asking Corazon to follow.

While they didn't really move far away, it seemed that they were miles away from the others. The air was crystalline with every small sound becoming magnified. Corazon noticed, with no small relief that the insects were gone as well. She and Sky moved slowly forward as the brush began to thin. They saw that the land was rising, but not naturally like the cliffs or a hill, it was more like a very deliberate upward grade. They weren't sure if they should go forward, but curiosity eventually overcame their doubts and they continued upward. They both became aware of an immense presence similar to, but very unlike the ancient trees. Always rational Corazon wanted to be afraid, yet was too full of awe to fall into terror. Sky was awed, but, being a Dog, took it in stride. They both wondered what awaited them at the top.

They climbed slowly uphill for quite some time. The grade of the hill seemed to be especially suited to a comfortable ascent. Although they did not even begin to comprehend how this had been created, much less why, they knew this was not the work of Mother Earth. As they went up and up, they became more and more eager to see what they would see when they reached the top. Meanwhile, the low humming that only Sky had been able to hear was becoming audible to Corazon now. It seemed to be a soothing and slow chant or perhaps even a conversation, but she still could not make out words.

For her part, Sky was finding herself experiencing image after image, each one with a distinct personality. There was a large and rather hairless dog with immense ears like Coyote's who was grinning, independent, and very playful. There was a rough-coated dog moving low to the ground with piercing eyes, braving the hooves of many sheep, making them move along with their People. There was a giant dog with a grey seemingly waterproof coat running in the rain with a pack of others who looked the same. They looked like agile ghosts slipping sure-footedly through the dense forest. He and the others were bringing down a huge stag, waiting patiently for their Person to come and take the meat home to their Village. She saw dogs like herself pulling a sled through the snow to bring food and provisions to others. She saw a dog smaller than the smallest puppy she had ever seen sitting in the lap of an Elder, giving comfort and love. She saw a man with no sight being guided by a dog wearing a strange harness. A dog quietly offering up the same dedication and purpose she offered to Corazon. She saw one of the Different Children frightened, kicking and screaming. A dog approached the child and gently restored that child to calm. She saw dog after dog after dog, and she wondered at it. She knew she was seeing the far past and the far future.

The two continued to climb the easy slope, each in their own experience. The earth sounded hollow under their feet, and they were both very aware that magic was all around them. Eventually, they stood together at the top. The view was nothing like what they had expected. They saw a long serpent of a mound winding and twisting but always heading North until it faded in the distance.

Corazon took a deep and somewhat shaky breath. She was too far out of her rational yet intuitive way of trying to control the day. She turned to Sky, wide-eyed, not sure if she was overjoyed to find a way North, or frightened by the age and spirits of this place. Sky did what clan Dog does best. She jumped up, leaving dirty paw prints on Corazon's already battered tunic, and joyfully licked her face. Sky accepted the gift for what it was, and Corazon understood that.

Together they raced back down the slope, eager to find the others. The Boy, Nika, and Coyote were more than ready to leave the heavy and dark forest behind, and they raced to the top with little regard for the ancient and future voices rolling around them. Only Nika stopped for a moment, seeing a vision of The Woman with a small and homeless Pup in a basket, and then a far-off future pup of Nika's standing tall and proud with ribbons placed gracefully around his neck while someone who looked very much like The Woman smiled down at him. He shrugged, grinned a very wolfish grin, and continued to bound up the slope, eager like the others to see the top.

63. North is Not Always a Straight Path

It was an easy uphill grade, yet when they all reached the top they were surprised at how high they had climbed. The breeze up there was cooling, while the insects had been left far below to search for other prey. The giant trees below them now seemed friendlier, and much less preoccupied with their own mysteries. All in all, the travelers thought this was a happy discovery. Corazon and Sky received a great deal of praise for their bravery in climbing all the way to the top. In their own way, they both blushed a little bit, not used to be the center of attention.

After a while of appreciating the view and the relief from the humid forest, The Boy noticed (as Corazon had done), that the serpentine mound twisted and turned, but for the most part went due North. Why couldn't they simply follow along this elevated trail and see where it led? By now, they were all convinced that coincidences were not always chance, and this seemed like an opportunity. They had all become somewhat used to the magic and the voices past and future rolling around, and each one felt that something of value was being communicated to them.

So the decision was made with little conversation, and they all set off along the top of the Snake-Mound (as they decided to name it).

Corazon, remembering her experience with the woman who went by the name of Snake was hesitant to call it that, but both a sleepy Owl and a very wide-awake Coyote told her the tale of how Snake sheds its skin and is reborn every year. While Snake can certainly be duplicity and lies, Snake can also be transformation and deep wisdom. The shadow-nature is always with us, but it can also help us to Spirit.

64. Walking the Snake in the Mist

Snake Mound was truly a magical place. The travelers could feel the age of it, but the mound was far from being a dead, cold place. It seemed that they were always hearing singing, or a far-off conversation that was purposeful yet filled with kindness. They all seemed to feel that they were being taught, although they did not understand what the lesson was. By consensus, they decided that this was a good thing, and they continued to follow the winding track.

Although they were moving steadily North, they were also moving westward, back towards the endless water. The Boy loved smelling how the air changed the closer they got. While the canids loved the forest with its constant sounds and life, and Owl loved the immensity of the night sky, and Corazon loved traveling with her clan around her, the Boy loved the water, the beach, and the rocks. He loved the scent of the air, and how the sand had so many different ways of being sand. It could be a hard surface for running, or soft mounds that were almost impossible to run through. You could create dribbling sculptures with it that would vanish with the tide. And the sound! The Boy decided that the sound of the water was like listening to the whole world breathing. The sky just felt bigger somehow, and made the Boy feel that he wasn't a Different Boy, he was a being who could do anything.

Truth, they were all happy to be out of the ancient and somber forest. They did not know what they were traveling towards, but really, who does? Every day is a bit of a journey, changing us. They were all changing, too - although they did not realize it. When you live with magic it gets into your mind and your heart. People see you differently. Corazon had become strong and confident in her magic. The Boy had become joyful in his. He no longer looked like a feral child - he looked like a bright and inquisitive Boy who loved his friends. Coyote was able to see the past as the past, not allowing it to taint the present. Owl had become both loving and wise. Sky did not feel that she had to constantly take care of Corazon, and was learning to truly live her own life. And Nika was growing into a leader. He stayed at the rear of the little band, always aware of the environment. He had a deep and commanding bark that the travelers had learned to respect. When Nika gave that bark, you stopped what you were doing and paid attention.

One day, on a day when they were very close to the endless water, they watched a mist come in along the shore. It looked like a wall made out of clouds from far off, and as it rolled in it became harder and harder for them to see their way forward. Coyote yipped in the front, and Nika would bark from the back. It was like walking in wet cloth, and everyone decided that it was time to light a fire and stop for the day.

They were used to moving along all day, and it felt very out of place for them to be sitting in the deep mist, watching the fire and pretty much doing nothing. Coyote suggested that they sing.

Clan Coyote is known for their songs, as is Clan Wolf. Nika suggested that perhaps they should have a friendly competition about who could sing the very best song. Sky asked to join in, too, as clan Dog has many members who are also accomplished singers. While Nika and Coyote were dubious, they graciously allowed her to join in.

The three appointed The Boy and Corazon as judges. They set to work making the fire bright and comfortable, and driving back the mist as much as they could. Owl awoke, and decided to stay for a while to watch this competition.

Coyote said, "Well, incidentally, just because we were discussing Songs, I have been working on a Song. It's about our travels. It's a story-song. Can I begin?" everyone nodded enthusiastically. Who doesn't like a good Story - especially if it's wrapped up in a Song? So Coyote began. He talked about finding the Boy, and saving him from a dire fate, teaching him all manner of things (at this, everyone turned to look at the Boy who was pretty self-sufficient in their eyes. The Boy shrugged and grinned. It was how Coyote said things, and everyone silently agreed to let him have his moment.). Coyote went on, with each adventure becoming grander and more perilous than the last. After a while, those listening no longer cared if Coyote's Song was the explicit truth or not. They were wrapped up in a magnificent saga with larger-than-life characters overcoming impossible odds. That's one of the talents of the Trickster. While he can trick you if you're not careful, he can also lead you into a story that is fantastic and yet believable. So they all sat, enraptured, and let Coyote weave his magic.

When he was done, he yipped happily. He said, "That was even better than I had hoped it would be! What a tale, what a story!". He looked around with a little smile, "And it's all true, of course." the Boy opened his arms and laughed, "Coyote! You are the best storyteller ever - and of course, I believed every word! Come and let me scratch your ears and give you a hug!" Coyote was happy to comply and curled up comfortably in the Boy's lap, ready to listen to the other two contenders, knowing that he had won the Battle of the Songs for sure.

Sky went next. Everyone knew that Sky had a lovely howl that seemed to pierce the heavens, but none of them had heard a Song like this before. Sky sang about being three-legged in a four-legged world. While it wasn't difficult, she sang, the hard part was People who looked at her as if she were less than Clan Dog. Or People who patted her on the head (like most of Clan Dog, she didn't like that, but People seemed to feel it was how one behaves towards Clan Dog, so she put up with it.), while telling Corazon that she was such a good person for "helping that poor Dog." She sang about having to work harder to do things that looked effortless to others. She sang that three legs was part of how she was in the world, and also part of who she was in the world. Finally, she sang about serving, and how Clan Dog had made a pact with the People to serve them. Sky knew that up there on the sacred Mound, there were generations past and future of Clan Dog who would hear and repeat her Song. She sang proud and joyful, while Corazon's eyes filled with happy tears that she was lucky enough to have Sky always at her side. At the end of her song, Sky was embarrassed, as we often are when we offer up our hearts. Corazon nodded, saying "Good work, Sky. Good work. Come over here and sit next to me. You are my true companion and I can't imagine doing my work without you!" Like the Boy, she held out her arms, and Sky tumbled into them.

Then it was Nika's turn. He had grown from a fuzzy little pup with ears ten times too big for his head, into a graceful and handsome young Wolf. Coyote looked at him from where he rested on the Boy's lap and felt a sense of pride and gratitude that he had been chosen to help Nika grow up. Nika wasn't Clan Coyote - he knew nothing about Tricks, and his Jokes were Thinking Jokes that it took one a while to understand. Nika certainly wasn't a part of Clan Dog. While he would happily walk side by side with his People, he did not answer to them. Nika walked his own walk. He was growing into becoming a Leader.

Nika's Song was so big that everyone was amazed. He sang about Mother Earth. He sang about how every day was an unfolding of a Plan that was larger than all of them, but was small enough that it fit right into your heart, where it would guide you and nourish you. It wasn't a Song that told a story, like Coyote's Song, or a Song about experience and history, like Sky's. It was Song that was like looking up at the stars at night and seeing how they rolled on and on, past what your eyes could see and right into the heart of Spirit. Yet you could look at a tiny seed unfurling in the nurturing soil and see the very same thing. Everyone felt that Nika's Song really had no beginning and no end - it was a Song that was part of them and larger than them.

When he was finished, Nika just lay down looking at everyone. They all looked back, round-eyed. This was their Little Brother? Their fuzzy pup with cloudy blue eyes clinging to Coyote's back? Nika's experience with the darkness had changed him, for sure. But not in the way the darkness had intended. Nika had become clearer, greater and stronger because of it. And there's the secret to Nika's Song so many can't see. You might think that the darkness has eaten you up and thrown away your bones, but if you're wise, you will see that it has made you greater, clearer and stronger.

65. The Song is Heard

Just off the shoreline further North, Khadja slept
fitfully. She never slept well these days, knowing
what was behind her, and what she feared might
come. This night was no exception. She would
awake from dreams that were all the more intense
because she was now sightless. Sometimes she
dreamt of others all over Mother Earth with the
same vision. She would feel powerful, connected,
and hopeful after those dreams. Then there were
the other dreams. The ones where she revisited her
hopelessness trying to save her village from the
fever that had ravaged it. She would dream in an
endless loop over and over - holding people in a
cold stream, trying to lower their fever, listening to
their ragged breathing, and burying too many of
them. Those dreams left her feeling that she had
not given her best - if she had, her People would
have recovered, and the Village would be strong
and thriving again. After those dreams she would
lie quietly in the night, feeling heavier and heavier.
Sometimes, she thought she would become so
heavy that she would not get up again, and sink
back into Mother Earth. At times, that seemed like a
good idea.

Mist plays games with sounds. Things nearby
sound far off, while things far off can sound right in
front of us. While Khadja could not see the mist,
she certainly felt it. Everything felt cold and damp

and static. There were none of the sounds in the night she had come to enjoy. No crickets, no nightbirds, no small rustlings in the grass. The silence felt tired and old. Khadja felt tired and old. She lay on her back feeling the dampness coil and unwind over her face. From a ways off, she could hear Wren's gentle snoring, and that made her laugh a little bit. Wren might be a mighty shaman of a Singer, but his snores were anything but melodic - however, she never told him that.

If you've ever lain awake and unable to sleep, you learn quickly that the night has as many nuances as daytime. Khadja knew them all. This was the time that she called "deepest dark", and while it is frightening for some, being the time when it feels that the night will last forever, Khadja found it to be a time where she could simply be. No expectations, no shaman's burden, no need to do anything other than be a soul riding the mystery. Sometimes, this time could bring unexpected answers to questions she didn't even know she was asking. Sometimes, it was a restful time that was healing, keeping her from sinking completely into Mother Earth and vanishing.

On this night, she heard the yips of a Coyote from what seemed to be nearby. Knowing the tricks mist could play, she decided the Coyote was far off. It was odd to hear Coyote-song on a damp and cold night like this, and her interest piqued. She sat up, wrapping her blanket around her in order to better listen. After a bit, she began to smile. This was no ordinary Coyote. This was one wise Coyote who was telling an amazing tale of intrepid and fearless Travelers overcoming impossible odds. While Khadja could tell that there was some Trickster magic in the story (she was pretty sure that Coyotes did not fly with Owls through the night sky, protecting the Travelers), she let it go, realizing that this story might be the harbinger of the Travelers she had been waiting such a long time for.

As the Coyote's tale came to a close, another voice came ringing in. Clan Dog told a tale that Khadja had never known existed, as she had little familiarity with Dogs. It was a beautiful tale about an unbreakable bond. She wanted to meet this dog, and she had an idea that seemed to come from nowhere and everywhere at once. Could a Dog help her move about more easily? She loved Wren like a son, yet she knew a time was coming when he would want a partner and family. That thought had often left her feeling bereft and a bit fearful. But here was new thought; could Clan Dog partner with her and help to be the sight she had lost? She shook her head, amazed. She even smiled a little, thinking of all the things she could perhaps do again.

The Song ended on a high piercing howl that rang through the night and almost seemed to dissipate the heavy mist. Khadja sighed, feeling like perhaps now she could sleep again. She planned to wake Wren in the morning and try to make her way to greet these Travelers. Granted, they were Clan Coyote and Clan Dog, certainly not People, but she did know magic when she heard it. She wanted to meet these two. She stretched, wrapped herself tightly in her blanket, and lay down again with a contented sigh. She felt much lighter in her heart as well as her mind.

Then from nowhere and everywhere, she heard the deepness of a Wolf's Song. It reached right into her soul and she found herself shedding the tears she had long ago sworn to never shed. Yet as that self-imposed burden was released, she began to feel a sense of unity with Spirit, and a sense that, no matter the horror she had endured, no matter her lack of sight, she still had worth and purpose. It was almost more than she could bear, yet she wanted to hear more.

When the Wolf's Song ended, the silence rang like bells. It seemed that the mist was lifting, and even though Khadja could not see the stars anymore, she could certainly feel them. She took a long and deep breath, smelling pine and rocks and the nearby ocean. She smiled again, looking forward to true rest and being ready for the adventure she was sure the morning would bring. Curling up into a cozy ball, she fell gently asleep, sleeping deeper

and more completely than she had in the many
years since the fever had taken her Village.

66. And Heard Somewhere Else

Redbird was watching the stars from the top of her favorite old Oak. Its branches were heavy with age, and its bark looked more like skin than bark. Oaks are the best trees for sitting and thinking, either far up in a strong supporting branch, or nestled comfortably in the cradle of the ancient roots. She felt the tree echoing a Song from far away, and she turned to listen as well. She knew that change was coming. With the defeat of Duck, new and darker news reached her now and then. It left her feeling as ancient as the Oak - and every bit as stuck. For all her wisdom, she was in many ways very young, and she had hoped that one stroke would remove the darkness from Mother Earth. But the more she watched and listened to the People, the deeper her sense of hopelessness became. It seemed that taking Duck out of power had only made some force she did not understand more determined than before to enslave the People and Mother Earth. Redbird knew that her thoughts weren't in harmony, but it seemed that harmony didn't exist anymore. So she listened, hoping something would lighten her spirit.

When she heard Coyote's Song, she smiled a little. Now, here was a true story-master. When she heard Coyote's rendition of how the Boy had been saved from certain starvation by him, she laughed a little, remembering how quickly the Boy had learned to catch rabbits and find good greens to eat. When Coyote sang about how he had single-handedly joined forces with a powerful and mysterious Being to create the Song of Ale and Mead, she laughed so hard the leaves on the Oak shook in laughter, too. She saw some of herself in Coyote. That lifted her sadness, and gave her a little hope. While it can be good to be solitary, it can be hard to be alone.

Then Sky began to sing, and Redbird looked down lovingly at Storm, curled up and sleeping at the base of the Oak. Although she knew he was sleeping, she also knew that one ear was wide awake, and he could leap to protect her in an instant. Storm felt her thought, awoke, and looked upward at her, brown eyes glowing with all the love for her that Dogs have for their People - or in Redbird's case, their touched-by-magic-People (and there are many of those, you just need to look at their Dogs. That will tell you.). Redbird gave Storm a silly little wave, and Storm grinned, showing his ferocious teeth. Then he sighed and went back to sleep as Redbird returned to listening.

Nika's voice made her stand up on the sturdy branch and listen with all of her being. This was what she had been yearning to hear, this was the voice that could help to heal Mother Earth. She was happy that Nika had found the Boy, and that the

Boy had grown deeper and wiser because of Nika, Coyote, and Sky.

She wondered idly who had finally won the singing contest, deciding it must have been a tie. She shook the cramps out of her legs and scampered down the Oak as agilely as a squirrel. Then she smiled up at the night sky, thanking Spirit for sending her answer. She snuggled into Storm's rough and shaggy coat, enjoying the familiar scent of her friend and protector. Like Khadja, she slept better than she had in many nights.

67. One More Listener

The Woman was also listening, and so were her Wolves. They sat in the night with the Songs swirling all around them and they smiled to hear such big magic. Coyote had indeed done good and right with Nika. She opened her hands, sending her love to Nika, Coyote, and her dearest Boy, sure they would feel it and know it was from her to help them on their way.

68. Khadja Sets Out To Meet the Travelers

Khadja was awake as soon as she heard the dawn birds begin to sing. She felt her way over to where Wren was gently snoring and shook him to wake him.

"Wren!" she shouted, "Wren! I heard them! They're on their way!"

Wren awoke, and was instantly on his feet. He knew how long Khadja had been waiting, and he was overjoyed to hear the excitement in her voice. "Should we go to meet them?" he said eagerly. "Or should we wait for them to come to us? What's the best thing to do?"

Khadja replied, "Wren, I just cannot sit here and wait any longer. What if they don't find us? What if they get lost? No, I know it's not practical, but I need to go meet them."

Wren reached for her hand, silently agreeing. He packed up some provisions while Khadja paced restlessly. He felt a bit of a song start to grow about how hard waiting is when you're not sure if your dreams will be realized. He needed to think about it for a while longer, but it had the feel of a good song.

In a very short time, they were ready to head out to meet the Travelers. They had no idea what or whom they would encounter, they just knew that they'd been waiting for a very long time for these beings to show up. Mother Earth was suffering. The People were suffering. Khadja, like Redbird and The Woman had experienced vision and after vision of endless wasteland and the People endlessly warring over it. She could feel acrid smoke from the deserts reaching into the forests. She seemed to hear children crying the monotone weeping of hunger that never ends. She heard the deer and the wolves leaving the forest to wait by the cool of the endless water for the buring to cease. Like them, she grieved. And she hoped that this vision could prove to be untrue. So, Wren had a song growing in his heart, and Khadja had hope growing in hers. Both fragile visions, but sometimes fragile visions prove to be the most tenacious.

They moved along the shoreline, Wren singing, and Khadja dancing in the water, kicking up spray. From a distance, they looked like a sort of celebration. The pale and tall handsome young man singing his heart out to the world, and the heavyset, dark-skinned older woman dancing like a child, her bright scarves flying around her like victorious banners. From far away, you wouldn't see the deep pain in Khadja's face, nor would you see the weary yet gentle compassion in Wren's eyes when he looked at her.

69. The Travelers Meet Khadja

Corazon was having a similar experience, watching The Boy and the canids play in the water. From far away, Sky was as agile as any Dog. Coyote looked like he had never had a care in the world. Nika looked large and silly, not a serious Wolf working hard to become a true Leader. Most of all, and what pulled at Coarazon's heart, was that the Boy just looked like a boy. He didn't look feral, he didn't look Different, he just looked like a Boy playing in the water with his friends. She thought about Rose, and all of the other Different children she had worked with. She wished all the People could see them the way she saw them - as beings of endless possibility - each one unique and precious. She had learned something from each Child she had worked with, and she had learned so much from The Boy. He had taught her about overcoming fears so that you could be part of a bigger thing. He had taught her how to stop thinking so much, and start simply be-ing. Coarazon sighed. Wherever this journey was taking them, it had certainly changed her. She smiled a little, while watching the splashing and playing thinking that it had only changed her for the better.

She became aware of some sort of movement far off and directly North. Corazon realized that it was the same energy she had been feeling to move them forward, and was ready to meet this new adventure. She called out to the canids, "Look at the horizon! There's where we're going!" They all turned excitedly to look at the small swirling of color in the far distance. None of them felt any fear - not even the Boy. They knew Corazon would not take them into trouble, and in spite of all they'd been through, they were full of hope about what this new experience would bring.

While they knew this meeting was going to change their lives, they also felt no sense of solemnity. They felt clear and joyful, like you feel when you just know you're on the right path. So they danced and played in the water while they made their way up the beach to meet Khadja and Wren.

Wren was singing about how the water went on forever and the Sun dropped into the water's arms every night, while the Moon rose to watch over the Earth when he first saw the Travelers approaching. He was so surprised that he almost stopped singing. What with Khadja's excitement and newfound optimism he was expecting something much grander and heroic than the sight that was meeting his eyes. He saw a tall and regal young woman carrying a heavy pack, dressed in a well-worn somewhat tattered tunic and deerskin boots. He saw a scruffy Coyote dancing in pure joy, leaping, twisting, and snapping at the waves. He saw a black and white three-legged Dog that was as sure footed and agile as any four-footed animal he'd ever seen. He saw a large Wolf running swiftly through the water, moving from friend to friend, always watching his Pack, even in play. And he saw the Boy. You could never describe the Boy as comely, that was truth. Not only was his mind different, he looked different - he was thin, and gawky with slanted eyes that wandered, his turned-up button nose, tiny shell-like ears and wild, wild hair. No, he was not comely at all but when all is said and done, he was beautiful in his innocence, his bravery, and his joy in his friends. Wren changed his singing to let Khadja know her Travelers were close, and he began to sing louder so they could hear that they were being welcomed.

The three canids, having much better hearing than their People heard Wren's song first. They looked playfully at each other, grinned their toothy grins, and decided as one to sing back. Their songs hung in the air like raindrops catching sunlight as they moved forward. Wren smiled to himself. While these weren't exactly the grand heros he had been expecting, they were most certainly exactly what was needed.

Khadja stopped dancing and stood waiting. Wren was telling her all about how the Travelers looked, and she could see them clearly in her mind. Like Wren, she had been expecting something a little grander than this, but she also knew that sometimes the greatest spirits were the most humble. So she waited.

For their part, the Travelers were looking at the odd pair waiting for them on the beach with the same set of feelings. A short heavy set dark-skinned woman dancing with abandon and a tall handsome young man singing were not exactly what they had pictured at journey's end. So they eyed each other until Corazon broke the silence.

"Hello!" she called out, "I heard you from far away, and here we are. We're not sure why we're here, but we know we're supposed to be here. Who are you? Why are we here?"

Khadja smiled, enjoying Coarzon's clear, calm voice. "You must be a Healer." she laughed. "I'm so glad, there is such a need for Healers now. And I know the others as well - the Child, the Leader, the Wise One, and the Trickster! You are welcome, and we have much to discuss. Come with us, and we will talk!"

70. Khadja Tells Her Tale and The Boy speaks Truth

So they all walked and danced along the shore until they came to Khadja's camp. She bade them to sit down and take the journey off of their feet, and they did. Travelers, Wren knew, were perpetually hungry, so he made a fire, wrapped some fish in seaweed and spitted a rabbit. There were some berries and some greens, too. Satisfied that his guests would be well fed, he sat back and began to sing. He told the story of the fever that had come out of nowhere and swept through his Village like a roaring fire, and how Khadja had worked day and night to save as many People as she could, eventually sacrificing her sight to the high fever. He sang about how even as a little one, he had felt the need to be her eyes - a need as strong as his need to sing. Finally, he welcomed the Travelers and set the little feast before them.

Nobody needed to be asked twice, and they all sat back, talked about nothing, and enjoyed the food. Finally, when everyone was licking their fingers and Coyote and the Boy were having a somewhat quiet burping contest, Khadja began to speak.

Because Wren had already given them the history, Khadja talked about what she was sensing going on in the present. Like The Woman and Redbird, she also felt that something malign was set loose and running about on Mother Earth. For her, it began with the sudden and virulent fever that suddenly took away most of her Village. Sickness was something she knew, but this had been so swift and so devastating that it defied her reasoning as well as her skill. She knew that Spirit always sends a cure along with a disease, but she felt this disease came from a place that could not be totally cured because it rooted itself into consciousness and became a way of living. Living in the kind of fear that always quickly hides itself into living in anger.

At this, Corazon jumped up excitedly, telling Khadja all about Duck and what had happened in her Village. She talked about Snake and Rose, and how Snake had been exposed. She talked about what had happened to Nika. Khadja nodded quietly - while the stories were new to her, the sense of disharmony was not.

The two healers talked for a long time. There really was no one-time magical solution. Mother Earth was like a person with broken bones - the bones would possibly heal eventually, but they would be changed forever, and healing was a slow and chancy process. Duck and Snake were merely symptoms. While one could certainly treat the symptoms, that did not treat the cause.

Then the Boy slowly rose to stand at the fire. While he would never be an eloquent speaker of the People's language he could, slowly and haltingly make himself understood. This seemed to be one of those times. He took a shaky breath. He was always embarrassed by his raspy voice and how mashed up his words sounded no matter how hard he tried. But he felt that this was important. He looked at his friend Coyote encouraging him with a warm look that spoke a story of love, respect, and friendship, so he began to speak. In halting and painfully slow words he talked about living on the outskirts of his Village and how he had experienced no love or companionship for many years. He talked about how he had been seen as a demon, less than human. He knew he did not look, act, or sound like other People, but when he looked at his reflection in still water, he saw a Boy, not a demon. He talked about how it feels when others see you as something frightening, inferior, and not one of Mother Earth's well-loved children. Then his strange eyes lit up as he talked about meeting Coyote, and Owl, and Nika, and Corazon, and Sky. He talked about having friends and how that gave him the courage to change - to go on a journey, to try and speak the difficult People-speech, to be more than just a Boy who was Different. Finally, he said that he had a little thought. Maybe, just maybe, the love, patience and understanding that friendship brings was a way to begin to uproot the poison weeds planting themselves in the consciousness of the People. Maybe learning about how to speak with the Animal Kingdom and the Tree Kingdom were also ways to heal - after all, one joke-filled conversation with a Coyote, or one quiet conversation with a Tree was more than enough to make you feel joyful. Then he blushed, embarrassed by his rough and halting speech and sat down abruptly. He hid his face in Coyote's ruff so he wouldn't see how the others were probably laughing at him and his strange way of talking.

The only sound was the crackling of the fire, and the Boy was sure he had been judged and found wanting. Then softly, so softly you could barely hear it over the fire, he heard a Song. It was Wren. Wren was singing back what the Boy had just said, and it was beautiful. So beautiful he could not believe that those were his words. But yes, they were. There were his words about his Village. There were his words about his friends and how he found the strength to change because of them. And then there were his words about his small idea. Coyote whispered in his tiny shell-shaped ear. "You need to look up, my Boy. I think some folks want to talk more with you."

The Boy opened one eye, peering up through Coyote's fur. He saw Corazon and Khadja looking at him with amazement and respect. They were shaman and healer with years of training and they were humbled by the Boy's small idea. Suddenly, he grinned, just a Boy again, not someone speaking power and truth. "I got it right? I spoke true? Did I do good?" He laughed when both Khadja and Corazon said simply that indeed, he had most certainly gotten it right.

71. The Question Presents Itself

Corazon and Khadja talked far into the night while the others slept. Both believed that some kind of action needed to be taken, but neither one knew exactly what action to take. They felt very small, and they felt the forces around them to be very large. After going back and forth for a long time, Khadja finally said, "Corazon, this is so much larger than us. I can see where I was hoping for a simple, magical solution, and I just don't see one. But, I have an idea. There's a sacred spot near here that we call the Navel of the World. Shamans and Healers have used it for generations to see their way forward when there doesn't seem to be a way forward. Let's leave the others here to relax after their journey, and you and I will go. Wren can stay, too - you can be my eyes. What do you say?" Corazon quietly agreed, although she had never seen a space dedicated to mystery, and she was a little intimidated by the idea.

They set off the next morning, leaving the others behind. Corazon had her bundle of herbs and tinctures, and Khadja had her crystals, smudge sticks, and various other shaman equipment. It wasn't a far walk and the day was pleasant. They talked about this and that and mostly nothing - both wondering what was going to happen, what they would learn, and how they could begin to help heal Mother Earth.

As the day turned into late afternoon and the sky began to take on a lovely, sleepy golden color, Corazon saw something reminiscent of Snake Mound rising on the horizon. At first she was going to point it out to Khadja - it was so easy to forget that Khadja was blind - but she stilled her hand, saying, "Khadja, what am I seeing on the horizon? It looks massive - and old. Is that where we're going?" Corazon wasn't sure if what she was hearing in her own voice was excitement or fear.

"We should be close." said Khadja. "Tell me what you see."

 Corazon described what they were approaching, becoming more awed with each step. "Well, it's like Snake Mound, but very different. It's layers and layers of rocks all fit beautifully together. All sorts of different rocks, and not rocks that I know. Some are shiny, some look like flat black pieces, but they are all very painstakingly crafted together."

Khadja sighed. "Yes, that's it. Wait until we get to the top. Do you hear anything?"

Corazon balked inwardly at the idea of standing and climbing on those rocks. It did not seem that People had placed those rocks, and she wasn't sure how they got there. She began to listen, and yes, there was a sound. It was more inward than sound, but it wasn't like the voices of Snake Mound. If Corazon had known about electricity, she would have said that it sounded like a generator, just waiting there with all of its power. Even though she didn't have the words, she could feel the banked-up energy. "Yes. I do. It's more like I'm feeling it, and my skin feels like the energy is rippling all around us." She stopped walking and turned Khadja to face her. Even blind, Khadja could feel the intensity of Corazon's gaze. "Khadja, you need to be truthful with me. It is safe for us to climb all the way to the top? It's overwhelming to me to even be this close to it."

Khadja looked back, seeing Corazon with a sight that was beyond physical sight. "Why do you want 'safe'? How do you learn anything if you stay safe, Corazon?" she said softly. "You've taken many risks to come this far. What's the point in being safe now?" She took a long breath and added, "You know that if you don't go to the top, I'll go by myself. And you will be left always wondering. Will you come with me - or will you be safe, Corazon?"

Corazon put her hands over her face. She had always felt that she was a cool head in a crisis, and she was. But in a crisis the only choice you have is to act or not to act. This did not represent a crisis, this was a choice. She was awed beyond fear by this place. She knew that no Person's hand had raised those stones, and she could not comprehend the vast power she felt from them. She was almost afraid that if she touched the stones, she might explode. She thought of the Boy and how many difficult and truly frightening choices he had made on his journey - yet he kept moving forward, he kept on growing. She knew what he would have done in this situation. He'd be halfway to the top by now, pulling Khadja with him, all the while thinking of the great tale he would tell at the end of the journey. She knew he would be thinking up his great tale to cover his fear and decided she could do the same. She would tell a tale of this day that would awe even Coyote. An idea began to poke through her fear. She thought, here's the plan, I will conquer my fear and turn it into a tale. She lifted her face, took Khadja's well-worn hands into her own capable ones and said, "Well Khadja, as someone has no doubt said before and will undoubtedly say again, 'Do you want to live forever?' Let's go!" And so they approached the mound and began climbing carefully to the top.

72. The View From the Top

After a time, Corazon became somewhat used to
the energy pulsing through the mound. It was easy
to find handholds, and the mound was a spiral
pattern - almost as if its creators had planned for
people to climb to the top. Khadja climbed steadily
next to her, agile fingers used to acting as her eyes
easily finding handholds. The afternoon was golden
and peaceful all around them, and they reached the
top quickly. As Khadja had indicated, there was a
dip in the top of the mound that looked a lot like a
human belly button. Corazon looked at it thinking
that while the mound's creators must have been
more than People, they did seem to have a sense
of humor. The sense of long-banked power waiting
to wake up was everywhere, leaving Corazon
wondering what the purpose of this place was.
Seeming to read her thoughts, Khadja finally spoke.
"Corazon. You must be wondering about this
place? What's it here for? Why are we here?"
Corazon nodded, again forgetting Khadja's
blindness, and then said, "Of course I am. I've
never seen - or felt- anything like this place. It must
have a purpose, it's not just a random pile of stones
in the center of a plain. Who built it?"

"The simple answer," said Khadja, smiling, "is that
we did. Our hands and our knowledge of the stars. I
mean that our ancestors did, and we continue their
work here. But." and here she grinned widely, "We

had a little help. You see, each one of us has at least one spirit guide. A symptom of the illness walking the earth right now is that many have stopped listening to or even believing in their spirit guides. That's how you get lost. Like the Duck and the Snake you've spoken of. They have spirit guides that are following them around, and their guides are weeping because they are not being heard. Some of the guides have come here to wait for new People. Spirit guides need a purpose just like we People need a purpose. Some of our guides are our ancestors. Some are from the Animal Kingdom. And some come from the stars. They're all mixed up together, but they are all guides. They helped us build this place, and many of them are here, waiting for the People to wake up and do the work the Creator made them for."

Corazon was entranced. She sat down on the rocks and wrapped her arms around her knees like a child hearing a great tale for the first time. "Khadja? What about People like The Woman and Redbird? What kind of beings are they? They have shown up so many times to guide us and help us. Who are they?" Her face was shining, all care and worry erased. She looked at Khadja, waiting to hear her answer, yet knowing it at the same time.

"We call them The Guardians." Khadja said simply. "They may have been People at one time, but they accepted Spirits' challenge to become more. Their burden can be very heavy because they move between both worlds and act to help us when we can't can't seem to listen to Spirit. There are many of them here walking the Earth. You don't always know who they are, because they don't often reveal themselves to People. Your Boy is well-loved by them because he also walks between the worlds, although he doesn't know that."

Corazon stood. Unexpectedly for her, she reached out and gave Khadja a hug. "Now, Khadja", she laughed,"I don't suppose you brought me all the way up here just to admire the view. I am thinking we have some work to be doing?"

Khadja replied. "Yes, we do. Time to get started." She made a circle of bright crystals in a circle around the indentation in the earth, then she struck a flint, and wafted sage over the area. Coarazon sat and watched as the Sun prepared to drop into the arms of the endless water and bring on the Moon to keep watch.

"Why are you doing that?" she asked. "I understand the sage, I use it all the time. But what do the rocks mean?" They're beautiful." And they were, picking up the light from the setting Sun.

Khadja answered, "You've seen how a cat has whiskers, and bugs have antennae, right?" Corazon murmured an affirmative. "When I use the crystals,

I'm putting out an antenna to pick up whatever energy is there so it can be amplified for us. Just like the Plant Kingdom and the Animal Kingdom has its own set of attributes - we can use the Stone Kingdom to help us." She resumed placing the stones in a circle, humming a little song while she did so. Even though she was blind, Khadja knew this landscape well, she moved with swiftness and authority. After a while, she had set a circle of rocks and sat down, facing Corazon.

"Now we'll eat, enjoy the sunset and see what the night brings to us." she said. Coarazon opened their parcel of food, sharing it with Khadja. Neither one said much, enjoying the play of late afternoon light on the crystals. Corazon felt her fear ebb away as she watched the Sun fall into the waiting arms of the endless water.

After the Sun went down, they unrolled their blankets and watched the stars. Each woman went deep into her own thoughts as they watched the play of the stars in their infinite field of sky. They watched the Moon move from the East to the West. When the Moon had finally set, and the sky was only lit by the constant stars, they went even deeper, each one feeling that they were one with something much larger and more knowing than themselves.

While they were both awaiting a dramatic revelation from Spirit, they fell gently and peacefully asleep, tired from the long day. When they awoke, they were filled with purpose and knew exactly what needed to be done.

That's how you know you're truly hearing Spirit. You just know, beyond any doubt at all what path you need to be on. Corazon and Khadja awoke with the Sun, stretched, smiled, and as one packed up camp to head back to the others. Neither one talked about their experience, but both smiled often like two people sharing a really good secret . They moved with joy and direction, arriving back to the others before the Sun had reached its zenith.

73. A Surprise For Khadja, and Corazon Tells a Spellbinding Tale

When they got back to the camp, the first thing Khadja and Corazon noticed was that Sky was off somewhere, and the males seemed to be unusually busy. Of course they had heard them approaching, and their sense of busyness seemed a bit feigned. Coyote was sort of bossing everyone around, the Boy was busily wrapping fish in seaweed for the evening meal, Nika was staring intently after where Sky must have gone, and Wren appeared to be in a smiling song-writing trance. No one would really meet their eyes, although they all said friendly hellos,but then going right back to their obviously important tasks. Corazon whispered in Khadja's ear, "I know they are up to something. They did something while we were gone, and they're not sure how to tell us what they did. You sit and be comfortable. I've traveled many miles with the Boy, Nika, and Coyote, and I'll get to the bottom of this." Khadja smiled and nodded, finding her way over to Wren, while beginning to ask him questions about his new song.

Corazon looked around, deciding to reach out to Coyote. Although Coyote was a Trickster, he also could not lie well at all. She knew that the Boy would simply close his eyes and refuse to listen to her, and she knew equally well that Nika would be loyal to what the others decided. "Hey, Coyote!"

she called, "Come over here and sit by me! Khadja and I have a tale to tell, and I want you to hear it first. Come over and sit by me." Well, Coyote looked around as if he didn't know his own name. He looked imploringly at the Boy, who was suddenly totally focused on wrapping the fish. Nika continued to stare resolutely out into space,and Wren seemed to be completely caught up in explaining his newest song to Khadja. He sighed, trotted over, and sat down.

Corazon smiled while looking at him intently. "Dear friend, I know something happened while Khadja and I were absent. None of you are very good at covering that up. Would you care to let me know what happened?" Coyote suddenly became very interested in watching an ant make its way in the dusty ground by his paws. "Uh, well, no, Corazon. It's a surprise. For Khadja. You see, Wren and Nika and the Boy and I were talking...and well, it's a surprise. Sky will be back soon. You'll see." with that, he took on the Boy's strategy and simply closed his eyes, figuring that if he couldn't see Corazon, maybe she couldn't see him. Corazon remained silent, and finally, Coyote snuck one eye open, just a little bit. She was looking right at him. He sighed, and opened his eyes. "Corazon, it's supposed to be a surprise! It's for Khadja! We want you to be surprised, too! Please just wait until Sky comes back, please." He gave Corazon his best Coyote-pup look, and Corazon finally smiled.

"Friend Coyote, it doesn't sound as if anything bad
happened while we were gone, so I will be patient
and wait to find out what this surprise for Khadja is."
Then she smiled a smile that was surprisingly
Coyote-ish, "Besides, I have my own tale to tell,
and you can just wait until it's time for me to tell it."

The two stood and walked back to the others, each
awaiting the time for tales to be told and surprises
to happen.

Corazon waited patiently to tell her tale. The group
looked questioningly towards her from time to time,
but she simply smiled. Khadja also sat quietly,
awaiting the right moment. After their meal ended
Corazon stood, stretched, and began to speak.
While she really had not intended to tell a grand
and dramatic tale of what had happened, she found
herself weaving more and more detail into the
story, all the while thinking that she now understood
Coyote's love of tall tales. This was fun, and
although she kept to the truth, she just made it a lot
more interesting. Khadja listened with a big smile
lighting up her dark face. She was also enjoying
Corazon's tale, and knew that it was laying the
groundwork for the task she would be presenting to
the group afterwards. She sat and listened with the
others wondering how many simple stories about
Spirit got reworked to make their message better
and stronger.

The tale went on for quite some time, and Corazon
was truly enjoying everyone's rapt attention. Even
Coyote had no comments as he listened intently.
During her story, Sky came back to the group with
another canid but she stayed in the shadows
waiting for her moment to arrive.

"And then," Corazon said, throwing her arms up
towards the sky in a grand gesture,"The beautiful
blue-skinned people walked slowly back up the
golden ladder into the sky, and vanished." By this
time, she was believing her own tale. That's the
power of stories from Spirit - as long as the truth is
there, the extra embellishments only serve to make
the story more understandable and believable, not
less. Face shining, and heart full of joy at her
accomplishment, Corazon sat down to cheers from
the group. They knew from listening to Coyote's
many tales, that some of what Corazon had said
had been spun from her imagination. Nonetheless,
they knew a good and true story with real power
when they heard one, and this story was indeed a
good one.

When Corazon finished her tale and sat back down,
Sky walked into the group. A young Dog was with
her. She was a beautiful light sable color, she had
big ears for good listening like Nika's, intelligent
golden eyes, and a lovely long tail that wrapped
around her feet as she sat quietly next to Sky. She

was beautiful, and all eyes turned to her. The Boy
just could not contain himself any longer. He had
been holding this secret inside all day, and young
Boys are notoriously not good at keeping secrets.
He leapt over to Khadja, who was listening intently
to the newcomer's small sounds and said in a rush,
not caring how his words sounded in his
excitement, "Khadja! This is our surprise for you! It
was Wren's idea, but we all helped. Her name is
Nungunz, and that means "North Star". Because
she will be like the North Star and help to guide
you! She is so beautiful, we know you will love her,
and she will help to be the eyes you have lost.
Wren got the idea from watching how Nika keeps
the pack together and how Coyote acts as our extra
eyes and ears when we travel. Oh, we are so
excited for you! Now you can go places all by
yourself with Star to guide you...." he became
aware of his garbled, mushed-up way of talking and
suddenly sat down, ashamed of how he sounded.

But the Boy's friends, Khadja included, were used
to his speech by now. Everyone had understood
him perfectly. He looked around in wonder, smiling,
and hugged himself in happiness.

"North Star", breathed Khadja, "What a perfect
name. Wren, tell me how you found her, how are
we going to teach her to be my eyes, and can she
please come and sit by me so I can see her with
my touch." Sky stood, and she and Star walked

over to Khadja. Star sat down next to her, and laid her head on Khadja's shoulder. She gave Khadja's ear a little lick, and Khadja reached out and held her very gently. Just that quickly the two became friends and partners.

Wren came, sat beside Khadja, and began to speak, "It seems this will be an evening of tales, Kahdja. I went back to our Village to see what I could learn about Dogs who help people. Our Village is slowly coming back to life, by the way, and the People want you to return very much." He stopped himself, "But that's another Tale for another time, and we will talk about that later. There is someone in our Village who has begun to raise sheep, and to weave it into beautiful clothes and blankets that are very warm in winter and help to keep you cool in the summer. The People in our Village said he has Dogs that help him with the sheep, so I went to see. The Dogs would tell the Sheep where to go and keep them all together. I saw this happen, and it was like nothing I've ever seen before. The Dogs and the Person worked together, communicating as clearly as you and I are now." (at this Sky, Nika and Coyote exchanged a glance and sighed a very quiet sigh. It would always be an amazement to them at how long it took most People to realize that Clan Canid spoke very clearly with Clan People.) "I saw the Sheep going exactly where they were supposed to go, and the Dogs watched over them." He stopped for a moment, took a breath and went on, his melodious voice turning even plain words into a sort of music. "So I asked the Sheep-keeper if maybe one of his dogs could learn to help you go where you needed to go, too." Wren suddenly realized how that sounded, and said, "Not like you're a Sheep or anything, Khadja. Those words just did not come out right. I'm sorry. Do you understand what I meant?"

Khadja nodded, stroking Star's shiny, thick coat, "Wren, you did well. I've had the same thought, but did not know how to carry out my idea. You thought it out, you found Star for me, and now my world can become larger. I will also have a companion to share the world with me while you can do other things. This is wonderful. Thank all of you. I feel like my life is whole again, I don't feel broken any more. Star will learn how to be my eyes, and to herd me as if I were a Sheep, because I can certainly be as stubborn as one sometimes. What a wonderful way to use her talent." By this time, Star, being young still, was exhausted from the excitement of the day, and had fallen asleep with her head in Khadja's lap. Sky trotted over to Corazon, turned around several times, and then did the same. It had been a long day.

However, the day was not over yet. Kahdja said, "Now it is my time to speak. I have had a vision, nothing as grand as Corazon's tale," here she smiled slyly in Corazon's direction, the two of them enjoying their joke, "but words that need telling."

Khadja took a deep breath, scratched the sleeping Star's ears, and began to speak. "This is not an easy tale for me to be telling. Like many others, I have seen our Mother Earth in pain. Too many of the People have walked too far away from what they know is the best way to live - in harmony with Mother Earth, respecting the seasons, respecting all of life, respecting the water, the wind, the Sun and Moon. Somehow, some of the People have decided that they don't need that anymore, and they can walk whatever walk they wish. Duck was one of them, Snake is another, and just as bad - she teaches that the Animal Kingdom and the Different Children are not part of Mother Earth, and not worthy of love and respect. Snake and Duck spoke what some of the People see as truth - not that we belong to Mother Earth, but that Mother Earth belongs to the People to do with as they will. Like any good mother, our Mother Earth is grieving. But she has also had enough, and she is not one to tolerate her children not listening to her wisdom. We don't know what is coming. Those of us who can see forward see only burnt forests, dry meadows, sludge-filled oceans, and the People continuing to declare their dominance. The Animal Kingdom and the Different Children will suffer the most - as long as the People refuse to listen. Without the Animal Kingdom and the Different

Children, the People will have no more foothold here, and they will slowly and painfully find themselves erased so that Mother Earth can begin again." Khadja wiped the tears from her sightless eyes and continued, " But, like any good mother, she is offering us a chance to change." She stood and reached out to the group of travelers, "You are one of her answers. The Holy Child, who is wisdom and innocence, the Trickster, who is stories that have power, the Wise One who flies high above us, watching all, the Leader, who rules with the Pack always coming first, the Healer,who does not think of herself, and the Wounded One, who is made whole through love and service. You are some of her allies, and your words and deeds can help to bring the People back to their true birthright. Wren and I will reach out to the People in the Village here, and we shall establish a sanctuary where all will be allowed to live and grow and love. We will teach others to go out and do the work you will be the first to do. You will always be welcome here to rest and then go on." she stopped and slumped a little, as if what she was saying was far too heavy for her. "This is not an easy thing I'm asking of you. There are more like Duck, and more like Snake out there walking like fleas on Mother Earth. But there are also more like Rose and the Boy, who are needing you. Can you do this? You have all come so far - and now I am saying that you need to go even farther. I would not blame you at all if you just stopped right here and stayed with us. But I think

Mother Earth needs you more than we do. Can you do this?" with that, Khadja simply stopped speaking, sat down heavily as if her bones could no longer hold up her weight, and buried her tear-streaked face in Star's fur. Star stirred in her sleep and gently licked Khadja's face.

After Khadja finished speaking, everyone just sat for a while. They couldn't look at each other, and they weren't ready to talk yet. They had all felt that what they were up against was large, invasive, and not going away on its own. Somehow the Travelers had felt that with ending Duck's reign and quieting Snake's lies, they just might have succeeded. It was difficult for them to understand that the journey was not ending in a joyful and safe haven, it was just beginning, and their only safe haven was a fragile one at best. Coyote hid his face in his paws, Corazon wept openly, Nika stared up at the stars, Sky moved closer to Corazon, Owl flew up to a nearby branch hiding her face, and Wren hummed a sad and quiet tune to himself. The Boy sat, stunned. He had no real knowledge of evil, even though it had always been around him in the way he had been treated by his own Village, and later by the People in Duck's Village. He had thought that evil, and walking away from Mother Earth's path was simply a sickness that only a few who were very lost succumbed to. Now he had heard differently, and Mother Earth herself was in danger. He thought about The Woman and him asking her

to be his mother. He had a fleeting half-formed
memory of Redbird, and felt a wave of affection
towards something he could not name. He thought
about his first friend, Coyote and how that
friendship had altered his life making him more than
he had thought he was. He ran long, agile fingers
through his wild hair and looked at his friends sitting
in sorrow all around him. He looked at his toes. He
looked up at the sky. Finally, he looked at Khadja.
Khadja had seemed like a thunderstorm of a
person to him. Unstoppable. Unbreakable. Like wild
wind and electricity. Yet there she was, crumpled
and small-looking, crying into Star's fur. Just like he
had cried into his friend Coyote's fur so many
times. In that moment, something within him
became whole - he was no longer a Different Boy,
he became a Person in his own right, whatever
differences he possessed were only what made
him unique and powerful.

He stood up, suddenly feeling himself to be taller
than he had thought he was. Maybe he had grown,
and it was time for him to see himself differently. He
didn't know, so he brushed that thought aside and
walked surely over to Khadja. He knelt in front of
her and held out his hands. While he had never
trusted his voice, always hoping no one would
laugh at his mangled use of the People's language
he realized that, at least right now, he didn't care.
He needed to speak, and he needed to make this

moment right. "Khadja?" he whispered. "Can you hear me?"

Kahadja did not lift her head, but snuffled an affirmative, holding Star closer.

"Kahdja, you are so brave. Not many People could face the vision you've seen and be able to talk about it like you did. You were honest with us, and now we understand the task in front of us. It's bigger than we thought it was, but we can try. We have to try. Just like you had to tell us. Maybe we can't do this - but we must try to do this. Because we are from our Mother Earth, and we love her, and all of her beings. We'll do this, Khadja. We will come up with a plan and set out. We will take this task on, even though it seems larger than any of us. If I've learned anything, I've learned that friends create a Village that goes everywhere with you. Please take my hands, Khadja, we are going to do this, we will do whatever we can do to save our Mother, and to save the People." The Boy spoke from his heart, and what he didn't realize was that in speaking from his heart, and in forgetting his impediment he spoke as clearly as any Shaman or any Healer.

Coyote looked up at the two and grinned. He was bursting with pride for his foster son. "You're right! We have some adventures to be going on, don't we? What tales we'll be able to tell!"

Owl hooted from her perch, "I can lead People to the sanctuary Village at night! Safer to travel at night, and I can see better than any Person in the darkness. I can help, too!"

Sky barked, "I can carry the heavy packs and make sure Corazon has all of her supplies to care for others. No worries there!"

Corazon smiled through her tears and said, "Sky, you are always my partner and my friend. I see my skills will be needed on this journey, and I am so happy to have your help."

Nika looked down from the stars and said simply "I will watch over you and protect you. I go where my Pack goes." Then he looked back up, lost in thought.

Wren leaned in close to Khadja and said, "Kahdja, you have your little army and they are ready. The Boy is reaching out to you, could you take his hands?"

Khadja snuffled and wiped her face. Crying is never a lovely business, although it is certainly necessary at times. She reached out in front of her, and the Boy caught her hands in his. "Khadja, listen." he said. "Maybe this will come to nothing, but I don't think so. We have magic with us, even if it is only

the magic of friendship. That's still from Spirit, and I
am thinking that Spirit knows what it is doing. Let's
make our plans and be on our way."

Khadja held the Boy tightly, and said, "You were left
without a mother, and now I am thinking you
certainly have more than one! Thank you." Then
she let go and stood up again. This time she looked
like the thunderstorm the Boy had always felt she
was. "We have work to be doing!" she said loudly
and firmly. "Whatever happens, we have work to
do, and it's time we were about it!"

74. There is Work to Be Doing

Everyone talked for a long time after that.
Sometimes, they were all talking at once, but they
were caught up in the flow of ideas and the warm
fire of hope, so they all understood each other
perfectly. Wren suggested that he go out with
others from the Village and place signs for those
who would be coming to follow - but to make the
signs a cipher,, so that you would only know it was
a directional sign if you knew what to look for. Owl
suggested that she do as she did on the journey
out, and fly ahead at night to see what the next
day's journey might bring. Coyote thought that
telling the story of Duck's Village (with a few
creative additions, of course) might help others
understand the danger that was present, and the
need for the People to wake up. Corazon thought

that she could do what she had done in Duck's Village and help to teach parents how to open the door into the minds of their Different Children, and she could teach healing skills as well. Sky and Nika wanted to work with the Animals living in the Villages, and help to teach them how they could reach out to People in very simple ways so that People could begin to understand them better. Khadja talked about training young Shamans at the sanctuary Village, and wondered secretly to herself if some of the Different Children wouldn't make excellent Shamans. She looked at the Boy and had a thought she put away for a later time. Right now, he had work to be doing, but later on, who knew? She shrugged and held the thought close. Right now she and Star had a lot of learning to do.

The Boy sat back and smiled a very happy and hopeful smile. He had no idea what his contribution would be, and yet he was just fine with that. He knew who he was. He knew he had friends, he knew he could communicate, and he knew he was loved just exactly for who he was. He did not need to try to be anything other than himself. That was enough, he thought as he watched his little Clan eagerly making plans and ready to walk into a battle whose outcome remained unknown. That was enough. For now. He felt something that he could only describe to himself as a sort of itch in his mind. The more he looked at it, the more he felt that he needed to be doing something. Like Khadja,

he decided to let the thought rest, and see what
time would bring.

75. Plans and Frustrations

The next morning, Wren, Khadja and Star set off for their Village. Wren and Khadja went to discuss how to make the Village a sanctuary for those who needed a new community, and they were happy that their meeting with the Village Elders went so well. Everyone was happy to see Khadja return, and they felt that the plan was a good one. Wren then went to supervise building new living quarters to accommodate those who would no doubt be arriving, and to talk about making signs to guide those people to the Village. He left Khadja with the Sheep-Keeper, where she discussed her ideas about working with Star.

The Travelers were busily preparing to walk back the way they had come along the Trader's path. While the unknown is always intimidating, Clan Traveler was accustomed to it and their resilience showed in their eager plans. Owl was already thinking about her flights. Coyote was creating his stories and wondering how to effectively reach the many People who did not happen to speak Coyote fluently. Maybe, he thought, the Boy could help him with that. He smiled, already enjoying telling the tale in his mind. Corazon was making tinctures, while packing her herbs and other cures. Sky was secretly watching Khadja working with Star, so she could make sure that Khadja and Star had a good start to their partnership. Nika simply rested and watched, happy in his role as pack leader. They talked little, but by now they were so used to each other that they didn't need to speak much. Whatever worries or fears they had were pushed from their minds - they knew they were faced with a gigantic task, and they had no time for worry or fear.

Wren and some of the People from the Village set out later that day to place the directional signs to the sanctuary Village. They had agreed on using a symbol of the Sun setting into the endless water to guide People West, and a Symbol of the North Star to guide People North. They also reasoned that these signs would allow People a way to get back on track if they got lost. After a long conversation, they also decided to set up an outpost right before the ancient forest that had been so difficult for Clan Traveler to navigate. Several People from the Village volunteered to stay there on a rotating basis to help others get past the ancient and inhospitable forest as easily as possible. Wren was both excited by the activity and proud of how well he had organized the People in carrying out his plans. He hummed a little song about how People working as one were so much stronger than just one Person working. Maybe, he thought, there was more to him than making magical songs. Like Khadja and the Boy, he wrapped that thought up in his heart as if it were a precious small child, and decided to let it rest for a bit. There was much to be doing, and Wren was eager to be doing it.

Khadja, for her part, was getting frustrated. Learning to speak Dog and learning to follow Star's direction was not as simple, or as delightful as she had thought it would be. Following Star's lead meant she had to let go and let Star give her directions. Well, Khadja was used to being the one giving the directions, and it was difficult for her to give that up and depend on barks, nose nudges, and sometimes getting her heels nipped as if she were a very slow and stubborn ewe . Finally, she just stopped trying, angry with herself for not learning as rapidly as she had hoped. She sent the Sheep-Keeper back to his sheep, and when she knew he was out of hearing, she simply began to cry wordlessly. Until she had lost her sight, she had always been the leader, the one who held control in any situation. Her blindness had taken her down, although she tried to not let that be seen, not even to Wren (who knew perfectly well how Khadja felt. He just didn't tell her that too often). She knew the reality was that her eyesight was never going to return. She wanted, no she needed, her independence back. Learning to work with Star was the only option. So she let herself cry out her anger at herself and her frustration with the process. After a while, she took a deep breath, wiped her face, and called out to Star, "Star! Let's go! We have work to be doing, and today I'm the

student and you're the teacher! No more tears.
Let's go!" Star, who had been keeping her distance,
not quite sure how to deal with the emotional storm
of human tears bounded over happily, and they
went back to work. Khadja was impressed with
Star's ability, and Star was impressed that Khadja
picked herself up and was able to begin all over
again. Slowly and awkwardly, they started to learn
how to talk to each other. From far up on a hill
where she had been quietly watching, Sky smiled a
toothy dog-smile and approved.

At the end of what had proven to be a very long day
they all sat down and looked at each other. They
were certainly very tired, but all of them shone with
purpose and the joy that goes with that. They ate a
silent meal, smiled at each other in appreciation
and as the Moon rose, they went to sleep while Owl
flew.

It's one thing to make plans, have hopes, look at
wishes and dreams. It's quite another to set them
into action. Some People only look at their dreams,
and few realize them. But, Clan Traveler, Wren,
and Khadja had done just that. Their dream was
now reality. By the next morning, the Travelers
were ready to go, Wren knew the Village was ready
to receive those needing sanctuary, and Khadja
and Star felt themselves to be a working team.
After several "until we meet again"s were spoken,

promises made, and plans talked about one last time, they were ready to set off.

Everyone decided that the Boy and Coyote should lead the way, with Nika, making sure all was well from the rear. After a few klicks had passed in relative silence, the Boy turned to Coyote and said, "Why did you decide to come with me? That seems so long ago." Coyote, instead of just jumping into an answer, thought for a little bit, then he said, "Well, I had no Pack, and you had no Pack. Besides, you were really like a big, hairless Pup. You needed me, or you would not have made it this far." then he grinned his biggest and best Trickster grin, "Besides that, I would not have made it without you, either."

The Boy smiled and scratched Coyote in that favorite spot right behind his big, dish-shaped ears. "You're right, my friend. You're right. Let's go chase down some new adventures."

Coyote looked back at the rest of Clan Traveler following behind them. "Of course." he said, "It's who we are. Let's get going. We have a lot of ground to cover before the Sun goes down."

76. The Boy Meets an Old Friend in an Unexpected
Place.

So Clan Traveler set out again, this time with
purpose and knowledge. They all knew who they
were, and what skills they brought to heal the
People and Mother Earth. They saw some
folks like Snake, a few like Duck, and many People
who were simply like the Boy had been, without a
real Pack to call home. Coyote told the tales (with
the Boy interpreting). Corazon taught about healing
body, spirit, and the mind. Sky and Nika spoke with
the Animals, while Owl flew on ahead. They were
happy in their work, and sent many West to the
sanctuary Village where they knew they would
receive welcome, and their Different Children would
be able learn in love and acceptance. It was work,
and not always easy, but they were all left feeling
like they were being exactly who they were
supposed to be.

Except for the Boy, who hid it well. That itch in his
mind just would not go away. He was happy with
his friends, who were his Pack, he was proud of
how well he was learning to speak People and
reach out to them, but something else was there.
He didn't really know what to call it, but to himself
he called it Magic, he was looking for magic. He
didn't even tell Coyote about it. He just kept looking
and waiting.

Sometimes he lay awake far into the night, letting his mind roam looking for Magic. He would lay there quietly, looking at the sky, watching the stars wheel in their endless patterns, watching the Moon rise and set. He wasn't discontent, but he wasn't completely happy, either. This night was no exception. He listened to everyone breathing steadily in their sleeping, and he thought about them all with love. He was happy with the work they were doing, and knew they had all come a long way from that night in the cave in Duck's Village. He smiled a little and then sat up, hearing a new sound. It was a song, and a very interesting one, because he thought it might be about him, or at the least, another Boy very much like him.

He decided to follow the song, and find out who the singer was. He rose quietly, to not disturb Coyote sleeping next to him and moved off silently through the woods. After a few moments, he saw the flicker of a small campfire and thought he maybe smelled roasting rabbit. Moving carefully, he finally saw who was singing the song. It wasn't anyone he'd ever seen before, yet, somehow it was familiar to him. He moved a little closer, not feeling any reason to be afraid, so he moved into the light of the campfire.

Redbird looked up, joy turning her harsh and angular features beautiful. "Hello, dear Boy!" she laughed, "I've waited so long to see you again.

You've grown up so well. I know you don't remember me. I made sure that you wouldn't find me again until the time was right." She looked back at the fire. "And so it is. Sit down, and let's talk. As you can see, there's some rabbit roasting, and if I remember correctly, you're alway hungry."

The Boy sat, feeling completely comfortable around this strange person who was neither young nor old, and who seemed to know him. "I think I know you. " he said in Coyote-speak, to see if she understood him, "I remember the not-dog, not-wolf, and you. You taught me how to live in the forest. Am I remembering this right, or am I making this up?"

Redbird responded in Coyote as well. "Yes, Boy, you're correct. Storm came and found you and I took care of you until you could take care of yourself and find your Pack. You've done so well. Now I know something is troubling you, and that's why you called me here. Tell me, I'll listen."

The Boy began to speak with her. He realized that, like Coyote and Nika, she could easily read his thinking, so he gave up on words and just thought. He wanted to do more, bigger, magical stuff, he said silently. He knew his heart was big, and he wanted to make it bigger, to tell more stories that would change People, to reach more children like himself who had been thrown away in hopelessness and fear. He wanted to talk with the

Sky, the Wind, the Water, and most of all, he wanted to talk with Mother Earth. He was happy with who he was, but he wanted to be more than just who he was. Finally he stopped, feeling a little embarrassed. Those seemed to be pretty big dreams for a Boy with wild hair, a love of wandering, who could barely speak to People. Then he decided that they were his dreams, and he thought he was ready for some big dreams after all he had seen and done on this journey. So he looked Redbird in the eye, and said out loud in his raspy, mashed-up voice. "Well. There you are. I know those seem like big words coming from a Boy like me. I'm Different. I know that. I know I look strange and sometimes People are afraid of me because of that. I know I forget to speak People sometimes and I growl and yip and howl like Coyote, and that scares People, too. But I also know what I see when I look at myself in still water, and I see someone who should have big dreams. Because I didn't die in the woods - you taught me how to live. I didn't get hopelessly lost on the trail, because Coyote found me and joined me. I was saved from Duck because you and the Woman and Corazon got me out of that cave with a little bravery and a lot of magic. I wasn't captured again because Owl flew ahead and guided us. I didn't get sick because Corazon kept us well. I learned about staying focused from Sky and how she works with Corazon. Nika taught me about being a true leader and how that's really a humble thing, not a grand thing. Wren taught me about how songs are magic, and can bring People together. And Khadja, " he stopped and sighed here, "Khadja taught me that being Different doesn't mean that I am broken, it means I'm stronger than many People are."

Redbird was still, so still that she looked like a statue. She stared unblinkingly into the fire for what seemed to be a long time, and the Boy wondered what she was thinking because she had closed her mind to him. Finally, he just decided to wait. Storm padded over and sat next to her, putting his massive head into her lap, and she absently scratched his ears. He kept his eyes on her patiently, and like the Boy, he waited.

Then she sighed, a deep and sad sound that seemed to rise up from the Earth all around them and to reach up into the starry Sky. "Dear Boy", she began, turning eyes shining with what could have been very old and held-back tears towards him, "You were so very small. I heard you crying from a long ways away, and I knew I had to help you. Because in many ways, you're like myself." At this, the Boy started. He was tall, and brown with black hair and green eyes. Redbird was small and pale with flame red hair chopped wildly (and the Boy thought, probably chopped by her own hands from the looks of it. That thought made him smile, despite the solemnity of the conversation). "Look at me." she continued."I look strange, too. You don't have enough words to use, and I have so many words in my head that sometimes they all fight to get out at once, and I feel like I make no sense. My Mother also left me at the edge of the forest to live or die, nobody really cared. I was too Different. I talked too much, and I saw too much that others did not see, or did not want to see. So I also scared People. Storm's Clan of Not-Wolf, Not-Dog found me, helped me learn to live in the woods. When I heard you crying, I sent Storm to find you."

She stretched, looked up at the Stars, and then looked back at the Boy. "After that, I became something that was no longer of the People. Somewhere between Spirit and Earth. So here I am, and here are you. I have my work here, lonely as it can be at times. And you, dear one, are looking for yours."

The Boy nodded so eagerly that his hair whipped around his head. He pushed it back with his hands and said, "That's it. I need my Work. Everyone else has theirs, but I don't."

Redbird also nodded, her chopped hair bouncing about as if it had a life of its own. "You've learned something important from each being you've met on your journey. That's a good start. And you've made yourself be brave when it would have been easier to give up. That's even better." Storm looked steadily at the Boy, and he was reminded of that frightening trip clinging desperately to Storm's back, not knowing where he was being taken to. He nodded, "I try. There's no point in giving up halfway through the journey, is there?" He smiled a little at that.

"And there's a third thing." said Redbird, looking right at him,"You don't even see giving up as a choice. I would say that's the most important thing. And now I'm going to tell you what to do. You don't have to do as I say, Mother Earth is always with us, no matter what we choose, even if we walk away from her. But you are like the Woman and myself. You are one of her Walkers-Between-the-Worlds and you know how to speak with Mother Earth, even though right now you think you do not. That is a high calling, and your journey has proven that you are ready for it. You are always going to be Different, and some People will be unable to see your power and your beauty. But many will. When you return to the sanctuary Village, there is someone waiting for you, and getting ready to teach you all she knows. Of course that's Khadja, you know that."

"You're saying I would be a Shaman?" the Boy said far too quickly for his words to be understood, although Redbird comprehended them easily. "But I'm just a Boy, and a Different one at that. Being a Shaman is complicated, and I know I'm not smart. Not like Khadja or Corazon or Wren are smart. I'm more smart like Coyote and Nika are smart. Doing-stuff smart, not thinking-smart."

At this, Redbird finally gave herself up to a genuine and very large grin. She hugged herself in her happiness. "Well, undoubtedly so, my friend. You are exactly what Mother Earth is asking for right now. She doesn't need any more People-smarts. Look where People-smarts have taken the People with folks like Duck and Snake running around like they own her. Look at what that energy wandering about did to your friend Nika, and how the Woman had to break her self-imposed rule about not interfering to help save him until he could save himself from it. Please, we don't need any more Thinking-smart, we need Coyote-smart. That's smart that can think on its feet, spin a good story and be heard. We need Wolf-smart that loves the Pack above all, keeping order and safety through that love, not through coercion and bloodshed. We need Owl-smart to see far ahead and trust the path of the stars. We need Dog-smart that serves People and loves People even though most of the time People make little sense to them." At this, Storm barked a very deep and loud sound of complete approval and licked Redbird's nose. He lay back, letting Redbird continue. "That's why you've been sitting here, enjoying my roast rabbit, darling Boy. Spirit is calling you, and you have some big work to do. You will always be my dearest Boy, and even though you started out with no mother at all now look at all the mothers you have around you. The Woman, myself, Khadja, Corazon - quite the army of women, I'd say, paraphrasing someone from a different time. Time for you to use your gifts. Speaking of time, now it's time for you to go back to your friends before they wake up and find you gone. And Storm and I have our own work to be doing as well."

The Boy stood reluctantly to go, tears beginning to form. He had just remembered Redbird, and now he had to be going. But he understood what was needed and started to move away from the glowing embers of the little campfire. He heard Redbird clear her throat behind him and turned to see her standing and smiling, "As they say somewhere else, 'but wait, there's more'...you know I have been watching your journey. Who do you think sang the Song of Ale and Mead? Of course I am not leaving you. Someone responsible needs to be watching over you, or I highly suspect you'd spend all your time gazing into tide pools and telling burping jokes with Coyote." her face went serious again as she continued, "You are going to be a wonderful Shaman, you will walk between worlds, and I will be there with you from time to time. We are more than just friends, we are brother and sister. Our Mother is the Earth, and we have work to be about to heal her. Of course I am not leaving you. Now, get yourself back before your friends awake. Tell them about your calling. I will see you when I see you. Again, a quote from a different time, 'Make it so.' " With that, she waved a cheery and rather silly wave, and put out the embers of the fire with sand. Then she and Storm melted quickly into the woods, almost as if they'd never been there at all.

77. New Journey, Old Friends

The Boy slipped quietly back to the campsite and curled up in his usual spot next to a very soundly-sleeping Coyote. He thought about everything Redbird had said, and then he decided to just listen to what his heart had to say. He was a little scared at the thought of becoming a Shaman, but then he realized that it was because he was looking at himself the way he sometimes saw People looking at him. As if he wasn't a whole Person, as if he were something less because he was Different in so many ways. When he looked at himself, he saw a whole Person. His friends saw him as a whole Person, not someone limping through life halfway conscious. Redbird and the Woman knew him to be a whole Person. Maybe it was time for all of Mother Earth to see him as a Shaman and a whole Person, too. With that thought, he hugged his first and best friend Coyote tightly and went soundly to sleep, ready to tell Clan Traveler about his new journey when the Sun rose.

Of course, we know what the Boy's friends had to say - they'd seen it all along, they were simply hoping that the Boy would see it in himself as well. In time, when they returned to the sanctuary Village, Khadja was happy that her dream for him would be fulfilled. Mother Earth, learning of the Boy's decision once more became delighted with

the Creation she felt had turned on her, and the
story continued onward from where it began.

Epilogue

There are many other tales to be telling about the Boy and his friends. There are many other voices waiting to be heard. You can see the tales happening, and you can hear the voices waiting to be heard, too. Just look around you. You will see the Boy in that Different child trying to make him or herself understood in a world that does not always wish to hear what they have to say. You can listen. You have a friend who is Coyote - someone who tells outrageous tall tales and questionable jokes so that they don't have to show you their pain. You can listen to them as well, because deep down, Coyote needs his friends as much as his friends need his jokes and tall tales. You know a Redbird, too. That person who shows up in your life and maybe says that uncomfortable thing about your potential that you're making excuses about. They're right. You're not too old, it's not too late, and the time is now. Your voice is needed. You know the Woman - that friend who is always there in the background. The one who can hear the small scared child hiding under your rational adult conversation. The one who can address that child's fears in a way that empowers the grown up you to go out and do the work Spirit intended for you to do. We know an Owl, too. The friend who can always see the bigger picture, and isn't afraid to find it all alone. And Corazon? She's everywhere you see someone helping others to be well,

whether in body, mind or spirit. Corazon is so
needed, and we sometimes don't see her wearing
her scrubs, comforting endlessly, and falling asleep
in a chair somewhere, waiting for her next shift to
begin. Sky and Star are there in every Dog you
have ever lived with, read about, or wished you
had, and they are true companions. Nika is there in
the fair and wise leader that is sometimes not seen,
but who is always looking out for the Pack. We see
Khadja in those whose bodies may not be whole,
but whose minds and hearts are clear and full of
purpose. And Wren is that person you know who is
always thoughtful, always dreaming, and always
ready to do the right thing.

Clan Traveler is all around you, as the story unfolds
over and over again in different times and places.
Let yourself find your fellow Travelers and begin
your own journey, with your own tales to tell. You
won't regret it. And you might just change the
world.